AN ANGEL AMONG US

I0666850

(A Collection of Short Stories)

J.E. SPINA

COPYRIGHT 2017

By Janice Spina

Published by Janice Spina/J.E. Spina
Cover Design by John Spina

All rights reserved

characters, places and events are products of this author's imagination.

DEDICATION

Anne Gillis Benedetto

To my friend, Anne Gillis Benedetto, who was an angel among us.

Anne was a kind, caring, warm, witty, intelligent, and generous lady with a heart of gold. Everyone who knew her loved her. She passed away January 3, 2017 before I could present this book to her. But I did send her the special story included first in this collection which is also the title of this book. Rest in Peace, dear Anne!

ACKNOWLEDGEMENTS

Thank you, my wonderful Beta Readers, Michele Rolfe, Patricia Bradley, Michelle Clement James, and John Spina, for working tirelessly to read and review my work and for your helpful input. Your assistance is appreciated.

OTHER BOOKS BY JANICE SPINA:

Pre-School to Grade Three:

Louey the Lazy Elephant
Ricky the Rambunctious Raccoon
Jerry the Crabby Crayfish
Lamby the Lonely Lamb
(Received Silver Medal from Mom's Choice Awards)

Jesse the Precocious Polar Bear
Broose the Moose on the Loose
Sebastian Meets Marvin the Monkey

Middle-Grade/Preteen:

Davey & Derek Junior Detectives Book 1
The Case of the Missing Cell Phone (Won Pinnacle Book Achievement Award & Readers' Favorite Award – Honorable Mention)

The Case of the Mysterious Black Cat (Won Pinnacle Book Achievement Award) *(Davey & Derek Junior Detectives Series Book 2)*

The Case of the Magical Ivory Elephant (Davey & Derek Junior Detectives Series Book 3) (Won Pinnacle Book Achievement Award)

The Case of the Brown Scraggly Dog (Davey & Derek Junior Detectives Series Book 4)

Novels: (under J.E. Spina)

Hunting Mariah

How Far Is Heaven

Table of Contents

AUTHOR'S NOTE

Thank you for purchasing this book. A review would be gratefully appreciated.

These short stories, written over a few months, were at first intended to reflect different seasons, holidays and celebrations but then my high school friend, Anne Gillis Benedetto, and I reconnected online after many years. This book became a dedication to this lovely, caring, warm, generous, intelligent and witty lady.

Anne shared that she had lost her husband over two years ago and then she had become ill with no chance for recovery. Over the next few months she shared her pain and sorrow but also joy that she would soon join her beloved husband, Dick.

I felt compelled to write a story for Anne to help her deal with the time she had left and to give her peace. Her story, **An Angel Among Us**, the first story, became the title of this collection.

Anne unfortunately passed on January 3, 2017 before I could publish this book. However, I did send her a copy of her own story and explained that I planned to dedicate this book to her. Her words of gratitude meant the world to me. She was moved to tears after reading my story and after reading her response, so was I.

I hope you will enjoy these stories as much as I enjoyed writing them. The genres are romance, grief/loss, mystery, suspense, sci-fi, fantasy, horror, and paranormal. You will find something for everyone here.

If you like this book please leave a review where you purchased it and share your review with friends, neighbors and family. Word of mouth is the best way to spread the word about books.

Blessings and love,

J.E. Spina

AN ANGEL AMONG US

Anne remembered that day. She had asked for nothing in return but when he came along that beautiful, sunny day on the beach, she knew she had found what was missing in her life.

Anne had spread out her blanket on the white sand and placed her umbrella to give her the most shade for her and her cooler. She had set up her lounge chair with the cup holder and opened her book with plans to relax but that was not to be. Coming behind her on the beach were her three best friends with coolers, umbrellas and all types of beach paraphernalia.

"Hi Anne, I see you got here ahead of us. Can we drop our stuff next to you?" Caren asked with her usual cheery smile.

"Hi everyone! Sure, I was waiting for you," Anne quipped with a smile of her own.

Shelley dropped to her knees and laid down on Anne's blanket. "I can't believe you didn't wait for us, Anne. The guys are coming soon. I told you about one of them that I thought you would love. His name is Richard but everyone calls him, Dick."

Anne gritted her teeth. She hated when her friends tried to fix her up with someone. She was perfectly happy to be by herself. She was used to being alone, and always found something to do and plenty of company with her three friends to keep her busy. Sometimes a person liked to be alone for a change. She sighed, "Really Shelley, I don't need a guy. Please don't do this. He probably doesn't want to meet me anymore than I want to meet him."

Janeen leaned over and whispered in Anne's ear. "Just go along with Shelley. She can't help herself."

Anne nodded in agreement and smiled. She knew she had to go along with this. There was no place to hide now. She would make the best of it and then the guy would never call her again anyway.

A short time later Caren came down the beach with four guys in tow. She was enjoying having all their attention.

She pointed ahead to the three girls under the umbrella and the guys followed.

"These are my three best friends, Janeen, Shelley and Anne. Ladies, here are the guys I was telling you about, Noah, Liam, Mason and Dick."

Caren had her eyes on Noah from the beginning and grabbed his arm pulling him toward the water. Shelley took the cue and got Liam by the hand as she headed him into the surf too with Janeen and Mason close behind. That left Dick standing there not knowing where to look or what to do.

Anne felt sorry for Dick and cleared her throat to get his attention. "Hi Dick. Nice to meet you. Sorry your friends abandoned you. Do you want to sit down and get out of the hot sun?"

Anne cleared a place on her blanket so Dick could sit. She settled back onto her chair next to him and stared off in the direction of her friends frolicking in the water. They seemed to be having a good time getting acquainted.

"Didn't take them long to get to know each other, huh?" Dick began.

"Yeah, I guess not. Listen, Dick. I don't want you to feel obligated to stay here with me. Feel free to leave any time. Okay?"

"Who said I wanted to leave? I like it here just fine, thank you," Dick chuckled and continued, "Caren said you would say something like that to me. She also told me that you have a great sense of humor and are the kindest person she knows."

"Well, what does she know?" Anne laughed so hard she cried when she saw Dick's shocked expression.

"Well, she was right about your sense of humor but what she didn't tell me was what a lovely smile you have and your laugh, well, it's delightful." Dick blushed a little but continued to focus all his attentions on Anne who was also blushing at this point.

The rest of the day and night were a blur for Anne. She had fallen instantly in love with this handsome, charming and witty man. They had clicked from the beginning. From that day on they were never apart.

Their life together had been full of love, laugher, fun and adventures. Anne's memories of those special times were precious to her and she would re-live them over and over again when things got rough. Anne and Dick were fortunate enough to have had many years together before he had gotten sick.

Many years later Anne sat on a bench overlooking the ocean not far from where they had first met. The air was brisk and the snow was soft and fluffy as it flew around her head. She thought over her life and smiled even though a tear glided along her cheek. She knew that she and Dick had had a full and happy life and for that she was truly grateful.

Time was slipping by now for the love of her life. Anne pulled her coat tighter and wrapped her thick scarf around her head and neck and headed back to the house. She wished she and Dick had moved when they first said they would to Florida where it was sunny and warm. They both hated the cold.

She slipped into their bedroom and watched Dick sleeping as his chest rose and fell in a rhythm. He was on medication to ease his breathing and it seemed to be working. Dick hated taking any kind of medicine. He wanted to be alert up until his last breath. Anne smoothed his covers and bent over to kiss his brow and cheek. She snuggled up beside him on the bed and soon fell asleep with her arm across his chest.

The dream came once again as it had many nights before but this time Anne gave into it fully. She and Dick were running along the beach holding hands when a bright light appeared in front of them. It was warm and comforting and they reached forward together to touch it. Dick's hands were larger and his arms were longer so he touched the light first. Anne looked up as Dick was pulled away from her. She cried out, "Don't leave me! Take me with you!" Anne woke up with a jerk as she looked over at the still body of her husband. Dick was gone.

Anne went through the wake and funeral in a trance as the myriad collection of friends came to console her. Nothing was going to bring Dick back. She hugged and cried on many shoulders as she tried to hold it together. All she wanted was to wake up from this nightmare.

Finally, the last person left the wake and it was time to go home to her empty house. Friends had offered to stay with her but she declined knowing that she had to get used to being alone again.

Everywhere she looked Dick was there in spirit. Her tears kept flowing. Anne turned to God and prayed. "Please God take me too. I miss Dick so much. I am ready now. My heart is broken and will not mend until I see him again."

Nearly two years went by but the pain did not lessen for Anne. She had so many friends who came to support her and try to help her deal with her loss. Anne used her time to keep busy helping others, spreading her wit and smile to cheer those around her. She wrote often online on FB and eloquently shared her opinions on sports, politics, and whatever popped into her mind. She always had a way with words.

One afternoon Anne felt herself running low on energy and sat down in a chair to say her daily prayers. A brilliant white light came into her room. It surrounded her and a spark of light touched her chest. She felt no pain. Hours later she woke up in the chair she had been sitting in when she had prayed. She felt her chest. It was warm and tingly. What had happened?

Week after week Anne continued to feel tired and couldn't put off going to the doctors any longer. After her exam the doctor sat down and spoke with her about the results. His face became serious, no more joking around as he usually did with Anne. She sensed something and smiled at the doctor trying to put him at ease. She felt light-hearted and not at all frightened when the diagnosis was given to her. It was going to be all right. She was soon going to join Dick.

Each day was filled with more friends as Anne progressively grew sicker. One of her closest friends designed a picture for her with a stairway to Heaven showing Anne climbing up the stairs and Dick at the top beckoning her onward. Her friend's kindness touched Anne deeply.

Friends continued to come from far and wide to help care for Anne as her health continued to deteriorate. Their aid enabled Anne to remain in her home. They were all angels among us.

Anne now knew that her time was growing shorter. God had listened and would be taking her soon. The pain was getting more intense but Anne smiled through it all and prayed. Dick was waiting for her. She would do her best to get through this for soon it would all be over and she would be with her love for eternity.

Anne wrote and expressed her love and appreciation online to friends up until she couldn't write any more. Then a friend took over the writing for her. Anne read all the letters from the multitude of friends she had touched with her kindness over the years. Anne's courage and strength were an inspiration for all who met her. She was loved by all. Anne's faith was what kept her strong.

Anne lay her head down on her pillow and before closing her eyes looked up at the ceiling. The ace of diamonds was still there. A magician friend had performed a trick for her and Dick more than two years ago and told them that the card would fall down within two weeks. Anne smiled as she remembered that day. Dick knew at that time that he was going to die and was convinced that the card wouldn't fall until he and Anne were one day together in Heaven. Anne reached up her hand toward the card and smiled as a brilliant light descended upon her chest.

Anne was found the next morning with the ace of diamonds in her hand and a beautiful smile upon her angelic face.

THE END

This is the actual card as seen on Anne's ceiling.

(This is the note I sent to Anne along with the story. Her words in response touched me deeply.)

Anne,

I hope you like this short story dedicated to you and your beloved husband Dick. May your journey be peaceful until you are together again. With your permission, I want to include this story in my next book, a short story collection.

With much love and prayers to you, a special lady, who I will miss! Your strength, courage, and faith have been astounding to witness. You give me courage to deal with whatever I am given. Please pray for us when you leave this world for you will surely rest at His right hand.

Love & hugs,

Janice Spina

From Anne Gillis Benedetto

12/27/16

Jan,

I don't know what to say other than one great big thank you! What a wonderful story! All of heaven is smiling at this one. I am so honored that you would want to include me in your next book. I have wanted nothing more than to be with Dick since the day he left. His passing left a huge hole in my soul – it can only be repaired by being with him once again. I love you, Jan. You have given me a gift beyond measure. If I were to sit at God's right hand, for which I am undeserving, please know that I would pray that you find the Fountain of Youth and Happiness for you and your loved ones so that you may continue to write such meaningful stories forever. Thank you again from the bottom of my heart.

Much love,

Anne

My response

12/27/16

Oh Anne, I am having a hard time writing this through the grateful tears! I wasn't sure you would like me killing off the heroine in this story but I am relieved you liked it.

I don't know anything about your life except what you have shared so I had to use my imagination in writing this. I am honored to know you for the beautiful person you are and will keep you close to my heart always.

Yours and Dick's memory will live forever in this book for all to read. Thank you for sharing a little of yourself with me. I only wish we could have been closer all these years, Anne. But I feel closer to you than anyone right now. I will dedicate this short story collection book to you!

Blessings and much love and prayers to you. Please tell someone to keep in touch with me about you. I know you can't do this anymore.

I love you too, dear Anne. May God watch over you.

Janice

Note: The original story that I sent to Anne was a little shorter. When I first wrote this story, I knew Anne did not have much time left, therefore I hurried to complete it to share with her. After reading it through I felt it needed to be a little longer. This is the extended version. I did not know anything about Anne's life with Dick but she gave me permission to use the story in this collection. I did not use any real names except for Anne and Dick.

Anne and I hadn't reconnected until 2016. The last time we were together was at our fifth high school reunion, many years ago. Anne reminded me that we had hung out together, shared plenty of laughs, and had a wonderful time. She helped bring back the memories to this forgetful soul. I hope you enjoyed this story about an incredible lady who I was blessed to know once again.

If you are reading this and knew Anne, please share your thoughts with me through social media or email and please review this book on Amazon or Barnes & Noble or wherever you purchased it. This will not only keep Anne's memory alive but also mean the world to me.

Blessings and hugs to all!

J. E. Spina

A LOSS IN TIME

She didn't see him as he walked into the bakery. She didn't notice the way he looked at her. She was oblivious of her surroundings, only absorbed in her thoughts. She concentrated on her coffee as the cream swirled around in her cup making circles as she mechanically stirred without really seeing it.

He moved closer to her table while he continued to observe her catatonic state. He only wished he could bring her out of it somehow. The accident had occurred over a year ago and she had recovered physically but not emotionally. If only he had not called his brother for help…it would all have been different now.

She drank down her last sip, picked up her unfinished muffin and deposited both in the trash before leaving the bakery shop. She never looked up as she passed by the observer. He reached out to take her hand but missed it. He shook his head and picked up his coffee and half-eaten doughnut and followed her out the door.

Gretinasha, or Greta, as most knew her, had begun to remember bits and pieces of her life after the accident. When she woke up in the ICU she was in extreme pain with her body broken and bandaged. She had cried out for help to the gray images that kept floating by her. One of these images bent over Greta taking her wrist in cool hands and running these same cool hands over Greta's feverish forehead. Greta sighed exhausted and confused and tried to speak but nothing came out of her mouth. These unspoken words stayed in her head trapped as she was in her broken body.

Days, weeks, months went by and she grew stronger in body but still broken in thought. She could finally speak a few words but then would get confused and forget words and their meanings. Doctors, nurses and other medical staff passed by her room daily and stopped in to evaluate her progress and offered words of encouragement. But one day it was as if a dark cloud had finally lifted from her mind. She called out his name ..."Drew!"

There was a rush of staff into Greta's room as bells and clicks could be heard of machines and other apparatus as they signaled their responses to her speech and renewed state of awareness. Greta was now fully alert and ready to move on but would she be able to handle what they would tell her?

"Where is he? What happened?" The questions flew out of her mouth now familiar with their sounds.

Doctor Gleason stepped closer and gently took her hand. "Welcome back, Greta! We've been waiting to talk to you for a long time."

"Long time? How long have I been here? And...where is here?"

"Here is...New York. And...how long...six months."

"What happened to me? Where is Drew?" Greta's voice was shaky and rising.

"Greta, I am Dr. Gleason, the doctor on call when you came in. I have been treating you along with many other hospital staff. Some are here with me now to say 'hello,'" Dr. Gleason took a breath before continuing, "Greta, you must take it easy now. One step at a time and you will be back to your former good health."

"No, no, I want to know now! What happened to me and where is my fiancé, Drew Baylor?"

A gray-haired, distinguished man stepped forward and replaced Dr. Gleason at Greta's side. He, too, took her pale hand in his as he began, "Hello, Greta, I'm Dr. Roman. Let me try to explain. You were involved in a head-on collision with another car. You suffered from two broken legs, a concussion, broken right collar bone and numerous contusions and abrasions. As for your fiancé, Drew, I'm sorry but he didn't pull through. Since he was driving he received the full impact of the crash. The person who hit you was killed instantly. He was drunk at the wheel."

"No, no, no! He can't be dead! We were going to get married on Valentine's Day," Greta screamed and tried to sit up and get out of bed but the myriad of machines was holding her back.

"Please Greta, lay back. You are not ready to get up yet. We need to bring you down for some tests and x-rays and then begin therapy on your legs. They are healed but not strong enough to hold you up."

"I don't care! I don't want to live without Drew! Leave me alone!"

Dr. Gleason ushered everyone out of the room and left Dr. Roman with Greta. After all, Dr. Roman was her psychiatrist and Greta needed him now. The staff continued to work with Greta and after two more months of therapy, both for her legs and her mind, she was released.

Greta moved along the sidewalk as she headed back to her small apartment. Opening the door, she nearly tripped over her cat, Pumpkin, named for his color and plumpness. Pumpkin followed Greta closely in hopes of getting a treat which she had already eaten. Greta found it was easier coming home to a cat than an empty apartment even if Pumpkin was aloof and only came to her when hungry.

The next-door neighbor had taken care of Pumpkin while Greta was in the hospital. Mrs. Cage had Greta's key and checked on the cat from time to time when Greta had to work over time or go on a business trip. Mrs. Cage had the tendency to overfeed Pumpkin which was the reason why she was so heavy.

Luckily for Pumpkin Mrs. Cage was observant and noticed when Greta didn't come home for a few days. She brought the cat to her apartment and called around trying to find Greta. She knew a couple of Greta's friends and her fiancé. When she couldn't reach any of them she called the local hospital and found out she was in intensive care. Mrs. Cage kept the cat with her until Greta came home.

Greta went into her sparse and plain bedroom and lay down. She felt exhausted from the short walk to Drew's favorite bakery. She went there every morning just to be close to the memory of Drew. In a matter of minutes she was fast asleep and dreaming.

They were on their way to Drew's brother's house to help him move into his new place. Greta laughed over a new joke Drew had just told her. He loved to hear her laugh and watch her green eyes sparkle with delight. Greta touched his face and Drew took his eyes off the road for just a second. Screeching tires, crunching metal and breaking glass was the cacophony that she now heard in her head. The next second everything went black. She felt herself floating and outside the car looking in at two broken bodies. She screamed and woke up in a cold sweat. She had remembered what happened.

Greta cried tears of relief at finally remembering that day. At the same time, however, she felt deep emotional and painful grief over her loss. If only she hadn't distracted Drew from his driving. She would have to live with this memory forever.

There was a knock at her door and her cat meowed to get her attention. Moving through a cloud of sadness, she approached the door and looked through the keyhole. She gasped as she saw Drew standing there. She pulled open the door and rushed into his arms. He hugged her back but then moved away as he came into the room.

"Greta, I know you think I am Drew but I'm not. I'm his brother, Darren. I went to visit you almost every day at the hospital but you don't remember, do you?"

"No, I don't...I'm sorry. I was in and out of a coma. I didn't see you."

"Your doctors told me to give you time before coming to see you once you awoke. I thought it was time now we met, we both have a lot to share about my brother. I miss him too. Can we talk?"

"Okay. I can't believe how much you look like Drew. I didn't realize that you were identical twins. He never told me. The only difference between you is your beard. Drew never had a beard, but it would have looked good on him, too."

"Yes, we were identical. Do you want some coffee? We can go to my favorite place."

"Where is that?"

"Oh, I think you already know…"

Greta smiled.

THE END

STRAWBERRY PRESERVES

Kim cried out in alarm as the sharp glass cut her index finger. The sweet strawberry preserves running through the cut made it sting more as it mixed with her blood. She looked around to see if anyone had seen her take the jar. She hurried along away from the crowds as she wrapped her finger with a wad of tissues to staunch the flow. She was angry with herself for dropping the precious sweet concoction. It was not like her to do something like this – take something that wasn't hers.

She thought back to her little son that morning. Seb had asked her to buy some jam for his toast. She promised she would even though she knew that she had little to spare to purchase it.

As Kim entered her sparse apartment she went to the bathroom to wash off her sticky and bloodied hand before going to see Seb. After wrapping her finger in a double bandage she entered her son's room. The sunlight was wrapping the cheerful room in a warm glow and bouncing off his brown curls as he played with his trucks and talked out loud about his adventures. Seb didn't see his mother standing there with tears of joy as she watched him. He was her whole world since her divorce. Her husband hadn't wanted to be tied down with a child and had skipped out on her. Kim promptly filed for divorce and moved in with her parents until their deaths four years later in a car accident. They were destitute and hadn't paid the mortgage on their home which was subsequently taken from Kim shortly after their deaths. She was forced to move once again to a small one-bedroom apartment which was actually an in-law apartment in a family's large colonial, for her and Seb. The family she was renting from were away most of the time traveling and felt comfortable renting to a single mother instead of to younger more independent and possibly less responsible people. Kim was happy to have found this apartment and hoped to find a job that would keep her and her son here and off the street.

Kim depended on a kind, elderly neighbor who lived in a lovely house across the street to watch Seb when she went to find jobs or do errands. Mrs. Jostens refused to take any money from Kim knowing the young mother was having a difficult time making ends meet. Mrs. Jostens made excuses to bring over extra food to Kim and Seb so she could help them.

Mrs. Jostens patted Kim on her shoulder when she saw her tears. "It's okay, dear, everything will work out. You'll see."

"Thank you, Mrs. Jostens, for watching Seb. I wouldn't know what to do otherwise."

"Oh, my dear, it's my pleasure to watch such a sweet boy." Mrs. Jostens noticed Kim's bandaged finger and some remnants of a sticky substance as she gripped Kim's arms in a hug.

"Do you need me any longer, dear? If not, I promised Sebby I would make him some cookies. I will bring some over as soon as I finish baking," Mrs. Jostens looked kindly upon Kim waiting for a reply.

"Oh, of course, Mrs. Jostens, you can leave. I'm sorry my mind was wandering," Kim tried to smile in reply.

"Is everything okay, dear?" Mrs. Jostens looked at Kim with deep concern.

"Huh, oh, yes, of course. Thank you again for coming over on short notice."

Mrs. Jostens watched as Kim sat down next to her son to play. She knew she had to help this lovely family more in some way. Mrs. Jostens quietly let herself out and went next door to her comfortable house, and picked up her old-fashioned phone and called her son, Cal. He would put her plan into motion. After talking with Cal, she set out the ingredients for her special chocolate chip cookies.

A week later there was a knock on Kim's door and a tall, handsome man stood with a briefcase in hand looking very serious. "Excuse me, miss, I am Cal Jostens, your neighbor's son. Can I come in and speak with you?"

"Oh, of course, please come in and sit down. I haven't seen your mother in a week. Is she okay? She usually watches my son a few times a week. When I couldn't reach her I had to bring Seb to my new job with me."

"Well, that's what I need to explain to you. My mother had a heart attack five days ago and was admitted to the hospital. Unfortunately, she passed away yesterday. She called me a week ago and asked me to draw up a new will that would include you and your son."

"Oh my God! What? No...I can't believe it! She passed away! She seemed so healthy for her age. How will I tell Seb?" Kim couldn't keep the tears back as she dropped her head into her hands as her shoulders shook.

Cal moved over to Kim and placed his hand gently on her shoulder for support. He, too, was having a difficult time with the loss of his sweet, kind mother.

"My mother talked about both of you often and expressed her love for the two of you. She wanted to share her wealth with you. She lived very sparingly and never spent her money on herself. She gave a lot away to charities for children and battered women."

"What? Do you mean your mother was rich? She never said anything about money. I know she wouldn't take money from me for babysitting…but I had no idea!"

"Yes, I know. There is something that you don't know about her. She was a battered wife and my father left my mother and me when I was a baby. If my father hadn't left, my mother said she had planned on leaving him to save me. She feared my father would hurt me. We had a difficult time at first, Mom said, but she used her sewing and baking skills and sold clothes and baked goods to stores and restaurants. She soon was doing well enough to move to a bigger house in a nicer neighborhood for me to go to better schools. She managed to pay my way through law school and then finally retired to her house here. Have you heard of Martha's Baked Goods and Clothes by Lizbeth? Well, my mother started both companies then sold them for millions. Amazing, huh? Her name was Martha Elizabeth Jostens."

Kim sat mesmerized by what Cal had said and took a few moments before she could answer him, "It certainly is amazing, Cal. I still can't believe it and why she never told me any of this. Your mother was always so kind and caring with both of us and never wanted to talk about herself. I feel badly that I didn't tell her how much she meant to Seb and me and how we appreciated the time she spent taking care of Seb." Kim shook her head and looked up at Cal with fresh tears in her eyes, "I am so sorry your mother is gone. I...we loved her."

"Come to think of it she made the best cookies ever. She was always bringing over a fresh batch once a week. She also bought Seb the cutest outfits and said she found them on sale at a price she couldn't resist. She must have made them herself. She was an incredible lady and we were blessed to know her."

Cal smiled after hearing the lovely compliments and feeling very proud and blessed to have had such a wonderful mother. He knew what his mother had sacrificed to put him through law school working day and night cooking and sewing and taking care of him.

Cal cleared his throat to get Kim's attention. She was crying silently and looking out the window at his mother's house. "Mrs. Rondo, I need to go over my mother's will with you."

"Oh, I'm sorry, Cal. Please call me Kim. I am still shocked over your mother's death. I don't understand why she would leave us anything. We are not family. She has you. You should receive everything."

"I don't need any of it. I am doing well in my practice and want for nothing. My mother would not even let me pay her back for my education. She insisted that I give it to a needy family instead, which I did. Now, let's go over what she has stipulated for you and your son, Seb, you said?"

"Yes, short for Sebastian. I named him after my father."

"Good strong name. Now, let me see. Oh, yes here it is. You are to be given her three-bedroom house and fifty thousand dollars immediately upon her death and she has set aside $200k for Seb when he reaches the age to go to college. This should cover all his expenses and leave him with plenty to buy a place and get settled one day in his own life with a family of his own. If any more is needed she has set up an account that I can draw from to assist you both."

"Oh my God! I can't believe this is happening!" Kim's face was white as her hands fluttered in front of her mouth, "I don't know what to say but thank you so much! You can't imagine how much this means to both of us. We have been struggling for four years now and I didn't know what I was going to do about paying the rent since I lost my job today."

"You are welcome, Kim. This is what my mother wanted. I have the check for you and the trust for Seb. If there is anything else you need please don't hesitate to contact me. Here is my card. It was a pleasure to meet you, Kim."

As they reached the front door Cal turned to ask, "Umm, Kim, would you like to go out for pizza tomorrow night? Seb can come too. If you have any questions I could answer them at that time." Cal shuffled his feet as he avoided Kim's eyes.

Kim observed Cal's nervousness and answered quickly, "Sure, we both love pizza. What time do you need us?"

"I'll be by at 6:00. Is that okay? Don't want Seb to eat too late." Cal smiled and his whole face lit up.

"Okay, sounds good. Maybe you can help me tell Seb about your mother." Kim returned his smile and thought, life is strange but as a lovely lady once told her, 'Everything will be all right. You'll see.'

THE END

A NEW HOME

One hundred Earthlings were chosen for transport, fifty women and fifty men. They had been carefully screened to ensure they were healthy, strong, and resilient enough to withstand the long voyage through space. They were Earth's only hope to begin a new life on another planet, Cerex.

The Earth was slowly dying from a poisonous atmosphere due to the excessive burning of fossil fuels. More and more people were succumbing to the effects of this poison. They only had one spaceship left that could house up to one hundred people at a time. Most of the Earth probably wouldn't survive when the spaceship came back to pick up more passengers in a year's time.

Lara sat in front of the screen evaluating data as it was fed from satellites around Earth. As an astronaut and pilot Lara had volunteered to be part of this group to inhabit the planet Cerex. She and many other scientists had been carefully reviewing the atmosphere of this foreign planet and had found it to be closest to that of Earth.

The scientists were dedicated to completing their findings in time for the flight out for these fortunate souls who would be venturing into the unknown. A year of supplies and seedlings from all kinds of plants and some species of animals would enable the Earthlings to cultivate their new home. Once the scientists calibrated their voyage they would enter cryogenically sealed capsules that would automatically open in six months' time upon arrival at Cerex. Putting the travelers inside these pods would enable them to conserve the year of supplies for when they reached their destination.

Trent leaned over Lara's shoulder to view the data that was streaming in. He was excited about the prospect of a new life on Cerex especially when it included being with Lara. She was trying to ignore Trent as she typed more data back into the computer. Lara was still upset over Trent's ignorance. He had flirted with another passenger when he thought that Lara was not around. A few of Lara's friends made Lara aware of Trent's indiscretion.

"Lara, listen. I know that I made a mistake. It meant nothing. You know you mean the world to me. Please look at me, Lara."

"Trent, leave me alone. This ship isn't big enough to separate us. Just go as far away from me as you can. I don't want to see you."

Trent walked away with his hands in his pockets and his chin resting on his chest. He couldn't get it any lower. Lara could hear him mumbling to himself as he moved further away. Lara returned her attention back to the screen. The countdown began and she pressed the warning button for all passengers to go to their pods and prepare for takeoff, minus 60 minutes.

Trent turned around as soon as he heard the warning and ran back down the long corridor to the cockpit. He peeked in, but it was empty. He took off at a fast clip to find Lara before she got into her pod, yelling her name all the way.

Lara was entering her pod as she heard Trent calling her. She stopped and looked around and watched as a multitude of pods clicked shut sealing in their inhabitants for the long journey ahead.

Trent was out of breath as he reached Lara's pod. His was a couple of rows away. He grabbed Lara's hand and pulled her toward him. "Lara, please, I need to speak to you before you go into hyper sleep." Trent's eyes were pleading and sorrowful.

"Trent, we need to prepare for our voyage. We have 45 minutes left now and it takes fifteen to prepare our pods. You must hurry."

"This is important, Lara. I…I need to ask you something."

Lara showed her impatience as she clipped, "What Trent? What is so important that it cannot wait until we get to Cerex?" Lara opened her pod again and began preparing it for travel.

Trent pulled out a small box out of his back pocket and got down on one knee as Lara's eyes grew wide with shock. "Lara, will you marry me and make me a better man?"

"Oh my God, Trent! I didn't expect this now."

"I was planning on doing it when we got to Cerex, but I couldn't wait." Trent's eyes were beseeching Lara's as he anxiously waited for her response.

"I…I want to say yes but I don't know if I can trust you to be faithful." Lara had tears in her eyes as she looked down on Trent and the sparkling blue diamond he held out to her.

"I promise to always love you, Lara. You are all I want and need in my life. Please, Lara, say something!"

"Yes, my answer is yes!" Through tears of joy she smiled at the one man she loved with all her heart.

Trent jumped up and carefully put the ring on Lara's finger and lifted her up into his arms spinning her around until they were both dizzy.

The countdown voice announced, "Twenty minutes till takeoff."

Lara and Trent kissed and parted as they got back to their pods and frantically punched in their codes before settling down for their travel through space. They both had smiles on their faces as they were sealed in ice that would last until they reached their new home.

Six months later the pods began to pop open one after the other. Excitement filled the air as each passenger got out and stretched and moved around to get out all the kinks from their long sleep.

Lara searched up and down the rows of opened pods until she came to Trent's. He was still inside. It hadn't opened. Lara tapped on the window trying to get it to open. Trent was smiling in his sleep unaware of her efforts to wake him.

Lara ran back to her pod and grabbed a tool that is used to open a stubborn pod. She pried at the door handle until it popped open. Trent still did not wake up. Lara leaned in and grabbed Trent by the shoulders and shook him. Still, he did not respond.

"Trent, wake up. Please Trent, please wake up. We are arriving on Cerex in a few minutes. I need you! I love you, Trent! We are going to have a wonderful life together." Lara pressed her lips to Trent's as her tears ran onto his face.

She backed away preparing to close the pod and send it back to Earth inside the spacecraft. Her love was gone and her heart was broken. As she was about to press the button to seal Trent into his pod for eternity he opened his eyes.

"Hey, what are you doing? Trying to get rid of me already? We haven't even arrived yet."

Lara screamed, "Oh Trent, you're okay! Oh my God, I almost sealed you in for burial later! I thought you were dead! What happened?"

"I don't quite know. But I do remember having a dream that I was being kissed by a beautiful Earthling!" Trent couldn't help laughing as he watched the shocked look on Lara's face.

"Trent, you scared me half to death! I was kissing you goodbye, you fool!"

"Well that kiss certainly woke up this dreamer. Does that make you my Princess Charming? What are you waiting for Princess; let's go explore our new world. We've got a lot of work to do before we get married! This contractor has a house to build!"

Lara gripped Trent's hand and followed behind the others as they walked down the ramp onto the brown sands of Cerex. Lara smiled feeling relieved that Trent was alive and well. Things were going to work out now that they were together. There was nothing that would keep them apart.

The new inhabitants of Cerex got busy immediately building their homes with lumber that was harvested from Earth. When they ran out they chopped down some strange Cerex trees that were stronger than any wood they had seen. It would suffice to complete their homes.

Everyone had a job to do and specialties that they excelled in. Until the buildings were actually completed, some of the inhabitants had to sleep in the spaceship. Therefore, the spaceship could not be jettisoned back to Earth to pick up more possible travelers. The builders worked as quickly as possible to complete their projects and stay on schedule.

Some rocks were found by the men out scavenging daily that provided heat and light. This was an important discovery for all since the temperatures did go down at night. The rocks took care of both issues making the dwellings quite warm and cozy.

A year later their settlement was established and their farms were flourishing with plenty of food. Life at first had been difficult but soon everyone had a job to do and things settled down. The strange thing was that there didn't seem to be any kind of life around, not even an insect.

Each day groups of ten men went further out to explore. They would bring back bits and pieces of vegetation, heat and light rocks and odd objects. But, they never found any life of any kind. This fact disturbed the group. They were still surviving on the supplies of water that they had brought with them but it would be gone soon and their main concern was finding more. They had to stop watering their plants to conserve their water supply. They could survive without food longer than they could without water. They dug in every area they could in search of a spring.

Lara was nearly full term in her pregnancy now as were many other women. The men knew that it was their responsibility to care for their wives and children. They went further and further away each day in search of water. Each night they would come back exhausted and fall asleep as soon as their heads hit their pillows.

A few days later Lara woke up before dawn in the early stages of labor. She gingerly got up from bed and stretched to ease her aching back. She quietly moved out of the room without disturbing her exhausted husband. She would try to relax and control her breathing and start timing her pains. After two hours she could feel the baby dropping. It was time to get the doctor. Out of the hundred inhabitants on Cerex there were a dozen doctors with different specialties, scientists, contractors, plumbers, electricians, and even though there were no computers, technicians.

Lara called out to Trent for help, "It's time, Trent! Please get the doctor." She took a deep breath and let it out in puffs as the next contraction began. Lara laid down on the wide padded bench Trent had made back on Earth. It was perfect for her with sides to hold onto and added support for her back. Trent had claimed it was a birthing bench.

Trent raced out to Lara and held her hand while he whispered words of comfort. He kissed her on the cheek and ran out the door to find the doctor. By the time the doctor arrived the baby's head was already crowning. Lara grunted and pushed as their baby, the first to be born on Cerex, came into this new world.

Once Lara was settled in bed with the baby at her breast, Trent prepared breakfast for his wife and new son. He felt love welling up inside him and flowing out all around him as he looked down upon them sleeping so peacefully. He placed the breakfast on the nightstand and left the room to allow them to sleep some more.

Throughout that day and into the next several days more babies were born keeping all the doctors busy. The men gathered together in prayer and Thanksgiving as each heard the first cry of their newborn. Once the cries died down a different sound could be heard. The men went to investigate and found a gurgling brook where they had dug a hole previously looking for water. The men soon scattered out to check all the holes and each was now filled with water. As they moved further out they found a pond beginning to grow larger as all the holes overflowed into one that soon became a lake. Soon the men noticed flying insects about their heads and lizards walking out of the wells. The water had brought more things to life.

The men reached forward and scooped up the water to taste it and found it fresh, cool, clear and refreshing. Soon there were celebrations all over the village not only to celebrate the births but also the newfound water that would provide for a long life on their new homeland of Cerex.

The spacecraft, which was sent back to Earth a couple of months after they arrived, never returned, for their former home was now devoid of life. Life would go on here for there was no turning back. Cerex was now considered their home and like all homes that are filled with love and children and laughter – there is no place better.

But out in the lake, the sweet water that brought forth life, reared some long-forgotten creatures. Home sweet home would not be home sweet home for very much longer.

THE END

END OF THE RAINBOW

Lily had always wanted to go to Ireland but was a timid soul and not at all adventurous. She used to dream about this trip and traveled to Ireland in her dreams. To Lily it was the land of all things green, leprechauns, and rainbows.

Hailey, Lily's best friend since college, agreed to meet her in Dublin for a week. They would find a nice hotel and then book a tour to see the sights.

Lily couldn't believe sometimes how different she and Hailey could be. How they became friends was a surprise to her. Hailey was more of a daredevil and party girl while Lily was content to read a book, write a story or just take a long walk in solitude.

This trip was an adventure for Lily. One that she never would have taken if it hadn't been for her cheating boyfriend. She had to get as far away as possible from Brad. Hailey didn't have a steady at the moment, but had so many boyfriends that she didn't remember who her present one was.

They were going to kick up their heels, visit some pubs and drink green beer and eat chips with vinegar, or is that in England where they eat chips with vinegar? At least that was what they planned to do. Lily had no plans to meet anyone while in Ireland but you can never tell what is going to happen in this magical place.

Lily sat at the airport in Ireland and looked around for Hailey. She waited for an hour and was about to leave and go to her hotel when in strolled Hailey on the arm of a handsome pilot. It didn't take her long to find someone, Lily thought.

Hailey was striking with her black hair, creamy skin and green eyes. She blended in well with the many Irish women who had similar coloring. Lily on the other hand had blonde hair and blue eyes and a sallower complexion. She never thought of herself as beautiful, maybe a little cute and passable next to Hailey's beauty.

"Hi Lil. Were you waiting long?" Hailey smiled at her pilot and waved goodbye as she walked alongside Lily.

"Where were you, Hail? I was waiting for an hour and almost grabbed a taxi to our hotel."

"Oh sorry, Lil. The time just flew when I was talking to Jaiden."

"Jaiden? Oh, you mean your pilot?"

"Well, yeah. Come on, Lil. Let's get a taxi and get to our hotel. We have a lot of sightseeing to do and pubs to visit. Can't wait to drink some of that lovely Irish beer. Oh, and I'm starving! Love to have some of their fish and chips, too!"

"Oh, now you are in a hurry! Okay, Hail. I'm a little hungry myself. Let's go. I'll take one of your three bags for you. I only have one and a carryon. What did you pack in here?" Lily exclaimed as she pulled the heavy bag along with her own.

They arrived at the hotel, unpacked and called another taxi to take them to a local pub. The one thing Lily and Hailey noticed when they entered the pub was the décor. It was like stepping back in time. There were tin signs, bric-abrac, mirrors, pictures of whiskey, beers, stouts, poets, writers, sports and beautiful stained glass. The ladies didn't know where to look first. They were in awe and loving every minute of the ambiance. Lily pulled out her cell phone and snapped away at everything.

After two Irish beers and a large plate of fish and chips, the ladies headed back to their hotel to book a tour for the next day. They wanted to visit Limerick, Killarney and Cork and walk around and enjoy the green countryside even if it rained. They brought umbrellas and raincoats just for the chance to enjoy walking in the rain. They looked forward to visiting the many gorgeous castles and the Cliffs of Moher.

After a tiring day of sightseeing on a bus, they decided to take a long walk and keep walking to get a feel for the Emerald Isle. The weather changed drastically from warm to cool, cloudy and misty. Luckily, they had brought the rain gear with them and opened up their umbrellas. They came across a large rock and stopped and sat down to take a breather. They had been walking for over an hour. They had no idea where they were. The countryside was rolling with a patchwork of quilts, now in green as far as the eye could see. It took their breath away as Lily once again pulled out her cell to capture the beauty.

Hailey turned to Lily and asked, "Lil, are you hungry by any chance? Because I'm starving! We have no idea where we are or how far away we are from any pub or place to eat. Maybe we should head back.

"Okay, I guess we should. But wait, look over there. It looks like a pub attached to a cottage. Maybe the owner lives and works in the same place. Let's go check it out."

Before Hailey could agree Lily went running ahead in the direction of the small quaint pub. As she got to the door of the pub she turned to Hailey, "Come on, Hail. Hurry up. Let's get a beer and a sandwich. I've always wanted to try some corned beef here."

Hailey hurried ahead and entered the pub right behind Lily. This pub was even more quaint then the previous one the day before and had the familiar stained glass and pictures everywhere of whiskey and beer but this time also leprechauns and rainbows. Lily snapped pictures of everything in sight especially the many leprechauns.

Lily and Hailey looked over the menu which was quite foreign to them. There was no corned beef listed but there was a sausage sandwich, banana sandwich, cottage pie, shepherd's pie, jam sandwich, a chicken fillet roll, and the famous breakfast roll of egg, sausages, rashers, black and white pudding, and sauce all squashed into a roll. Both ladies settled on the chicken fillet roll which sounded somewhat American.

"Really Lil, do you believe in leprechauns and a pot of gold? Is that why you wanted to come to Ireland to follow a rainbow to its end and pick up your gold?" Hailey chuckled at her friend's interest in such silly things.

"Don't you believe just a little, Hail? You never know. Have you ever followed a rainbow to the end?"

"No, and I don't plan to either. I can think of a dozen things much more interesting to do. Come on, Lil, sit down and eat your sandwich and beer. The sandwich is getting cold and the beer is getting warm, or at least warmer."

While the ladies sat enjoying their lunch, two Irish gentlemen were admiring them. The men whispered back and forth between them discussing the lovely ladies and how they would introduce themselves and maybe get lucky.

Hailey noticed the two gentlemen and their interest in her and Lily but she did not feel the same about them. She nudged Lily and urged her to hurry up and finish her beer.

"Lily, don't look now but those two guys at the bar are going to come over here. They have been whispering about us. I don't particularly like the looks of them. They are probably drunk."

Lily swallowed down the last swig of beer, wiped her mouth and grabbed her cell phone, raincoat and umbrella and followed close behind Hailey as she headed out of the pub.

As soon as the door shut behind them, it opened again and the two men stuck their heads out and called, "Good afternoon to ye, ladies. Would you like another beer?" They both had red curly hair, freckles on their faces and crinkles next to their eyes from all the smiling they evidently did. They were wearing their best smiles now, with a few teeth missing, just for the ladies.

"Oh, no thank you, gentlemen. We have had enough and need to get back to our husbands. Good day to ye," Hailey said imitating the men's speech as she pulled Lily along to make haste and get away before the men came out and followed them.

"Why did you tell them that we were married?"

"Well did you see them, Lily? They were quite a sight. I hope not all Irishmen look like them."

The ladies chuckled all the way back to their hotel. Upon arrival, they retired to their room to freshen up and find a place to go for dinner. Lily called down to the concierge for a suggestion of where they should dine. He had several places to recommend and told Lily to check the book that was on the table in their room for menus. Hailey perused the menus and eliminated several right away leaving only a few for Lily to choose from.

"What was wrong with all the others, Hail? Wait a minute, they didn't have fish and chips or green beer?" Lily smirked as she flipped through the rest of the book. "You aren't going to find green beer here, Hail. That is only in America. You will have to settle for dark Irish beer."

"Aw you burst my bubble, Lil. I was looking forward to some green beer. Well, I hope we can get fish and chips."

"Well, which restaurant did you choose, Lil? We should make a reservation. I'll call the concierge. Show me which one you like."

"This one sounds good. Yep, it has fish and chips. They have a little of this and that. We should be able to find something to eat. What time do you want to go?"

"Seven is good. We can walk around town afterward and get a flair for the people here. I love to listen to their accents.'

"To them, we have accents too, Hail."

"Yeah, I guess you're right. Never thought of that before."

Lily chirped up, "I would like to see the Blarney Stone. You know you are supposed to kiss it for good luck, I think. Although the idea of kissing a stone that millions of

others have kissed doesn't sound too exciting or sanitary."
Lily got a funny look on her face as she said this.

"Oh Lil, now I know why you wanted to come here. You want to make a wish and kiss the Blarney Stone and then find a rainbow and pick up your pot of gold and maybe a handsome Irish lad too." Hailey laughed out loud until she cried.

"Very funny, Hail! All those millions of people who come here must believe it too!" Lily harrumphed and went into the bathroom to freshen up and put on her makeup and sulk a little.

"Oh come on, Lil. I was only kidding. I want to see the Blarney Stone too. Maybe we can fit it in tomorrow as part of a tour."

Lily came out of the bathroom when she heard what Hailey had to say. "Are you sure, Hail? I don't want you to do anything you don't want to do while we are here. I can always go by myself."

"No way, Lil. I want to be around when you find your pot of gold and your dreamboat." Hailey smiled as she brushed her hair and applied her makeup and gave Lily a wink.

Dinner that night was uneventful but interesting. The ladies spent the time listening to the conversations and lilting accents of the locals. Lily snapped pics of some of them while Hailey checked out the local lads for prospects. They were also checking her out.

Lily had had enough beer, taken hundreds of photos, and was yawning as she excused herself to go to the ladies' room. The bathroom was tiny and the sink had two faucets, separated, one for hot and one for cold. Never shall two meet in the middle. This made it difficult to thoroughly wash your hands without either freezing or burning them simultaneously. Lily did a quick job of it and went back to find Hailey sitting at the bar with four strapping lads in rapturous conversation. It was going to be a long night, Lily thought.

Lily sat at their table and scanned through her photos while keeping an eye out for Hailey to finish up her conversation. Hopefully, Hailey would get the hint that Lily was waiting for her as patiently as she could. Hailey looked over at Lily and raised her hand with two fingers extended indicating that she needed two more minutes. Lily nodded and went back to her phone.

Unbeknownst to Lily, she was being observed by one of the gentlemen further down at the bar. He had noticed her the minute she had stepped into the restaurant. He was listening to the conversation of the attractive woman at the bar and overheard that the two ladies were going to see the Blarney Stone the next day. He hadn't been there in a long time and thought it was time to visit again.

As the observer passed by his friends at the bar they called out to him, "Hey Padraig, where are you going? Need your beauty sleep, do ye?" Guffaws and chuckles followed him out the door.

A half hour later the ladies were back at their hotel and relaxing with coffees and a pieces of rhubarb crumble cake. The hotel had so many desserts to choose from but this one was not as sweet and filling as some of the other choices. Licking their lips and picking up the delectable crumbs from their plates they discussed what they would be doing on their tour in the morning.

Lily scrolled on her phone and found Blarney Stone. It said, the Blarney Stone is a block of carboniferous limestone built into the battlements of Blarney Castle in Blarney. According to legend, kissing the stone bestowed upon the kisser a gift of eloquence or the ability to flatter. The word blarney in the dictionary means skillful flattery, blandishment, nonsense, humbug.

"Hailey, I don't think you need to kiss the stone. You didn't have any trouble talking to those Irish lads at the restaurant tonight. I am the one that gets tongue tied and nervous around men. I need all the help I can get. I better kiss it twice!" Lily laughed at her own humor.

"Ha, you may have to, Lily. But all you need to do is relax and think of all men in their underwear. That will give you the upper hand right from the start. Men are not frightening creatures to begin with. I learned at an early age how to wrap men around my little finger. My dad would give me anything I wanted. All I had to do was mention how lovely something was and he would buy it for me. It drove my mother crazy!" Hailey smiled as she winked at Lily.

"Oh, Hailey, you are incorrigible! Your poor mother couldn't compete with you. I feel sorry for your dad too.

He didn't know what hit him when you were born!" The ladies giggled like school girls.

The tour was full of people from all nations which was evident by the multitude of languages being spoken at once. Hailey somehow managed to get into conversation with a handsome Italian man who moved away from his group to sit next to her.

Lily opened her phone to again read up on the Blarney Stone and Blarney Castle. She planned to share some of this information with Hailey, but by the looks of her friend, she wouldn't be interested. Hailey had other things in mind.

Upon further reading, Lily found out that the ritual of kissing the Blarney Stone had been done by millions of people from all over the world. There were guide rails to hold onto now which made it a lot safer to do. At one time people had to lean over backwards and hopefully have someone hold onto their feet to keep them from falling to their deaths.

It was amazing that people risked life and limb to kiss this Stone. *I certainly wouldn't have been as brave*, thought

Lily. She sighed and looked over at Hailey who was talking non-stop to the Italian gentleman, who appeared to be enchanted by her every word. Hailey definitely had the gift of gab. *If only I could be half as articulate with the opposite sex, I would be happy.*

The bus stopped outside Blarney Castle and everyone was off before Hailey even moved to stand up. She was so involved in her conversation with her latest boyfriend. The Italian gentlemen offered his arm to Hailey and escorted her off the bus as Lily waited along with the rest of the tourists for her majesty to make an appearance.

It appears that I am on my own on this tour since Hailey is hanging onto this new man in her life for fear he may disappear. Hailey turned to Lily when she noticed the disappointment on her friend's face.

"Hey Lil, come along with us. This is Alessio, my new friend. Alessio, this is Lily, my best friend. Okay now that you know each other let's go see this Blarney Stone and bestow our kisses and then go eat."

Lily shook hands with Alessio who had the softest hands of any man she knew. Alessio bent forward and kissed her hand and smiled but quickly returned all his attention back to Hailey.

Lily followed behind them while listening to the guide tell them about the Blarney Stone. She had studied up on the Stone the night before and again this morning and could almost recite it back by rote. Lily was excited to see the Stone and eventually lay her own kiss upon its stone-cold surface.

Standing along the side of the group was Padraig who had been there waiting for a glimpse of the lovely lady he had seen at the pub the night before. Once he spotted her he pushed his way toward her and walked alongside casually bumping into her.

"Oh, please excuse me, miss. I didn't mean to bump into you. It's busy today. I guess there are a lot of people who want to experience the loquaciousness after a kiss."

Padraig reached out his hand and introduced himself. "Hi, I'm Padraig."

"Oh, hi Padraig. I'm Lily." Lily was feeling anxious just saying that. She looked up at this tall, handsome Irishman with a mop of curly black hair and felt her heart go aflutter. *Why is he talking to me?*

"It's nice to meet you. Are you okay, Lily?" Padraig leaned down to Lily's height of 5' 3" from his of 6' 2".

Lily felt faint once she saw how green his eyes were as he got closer. She couldn't speak and just stuttered, "I...I'm okay, thank you." Lily closed her eyes and took a deep breath. When she opened her eyes, she was standing in front of the Blarney Stone. Padraig assisted her as she bent backwards and held onto the bars to kiss the Stone. She was lifted by this magnificent man as if she didn't weigh an ounce. His arms were still around her as he settled her down on her feet.

Lily felt something extraordinary as she stood up. She actually could speak again without stuttering. "Thank you, kind sir, for your help. I don't think I would have been able to do that without you." Lily smiled widely at Padraig.

Padraig bowed and said, "At your service, dear lady. It was my pleasure."

Hailey rushed over to Lily when she saw her with a man. "Lily, who is your friend?" Hailey said as she batted her eyes at Padraig while Alessio frowned beside her.

"This is Padraig. Padraig, meet my best friend, Hailey, and her friend, Alessio."

Hands were shook all around as Padraig returned his attentions to Lily to her surprise and delight. Padraig, guided Lily over to an area free of tourists and asked her, "Lily, would you like to go out to dinner with me tonight? If you would like to invite your friends too that would be fine."

Hailey was keeping her eyes on Lily and leaned in to listen. "Oh, we would love to go out to dinner with you and Lily. Wouldn't we, Alessio?" Alessio nodded not looking too pleased however.

"Is that a yes from you too, Lily?"

Lily smiled and answered, "Yes, I would like that very much."

"Wonderful! I will make reservations and come pick you up at your hotel once I know which hotel that is."

Alessio finally spoke, "I will pick up Hailey and meet you both there once I know which restaurant." Padraig nodded and shook hands with Alessio as Alessio turned toward Hailey again.

"We are heading back to the hotel now, Lily. Do you and Padraig want to come?"

Lily didn't know how to answer that and looked at Padraig for some help. "No, I will take Lily back to her hotel later, thank you. If that is all right with her, Lily?"

"Oh, okay, Padraig." Lily smiled shocked at her bravado of trusting a strange man in a foreign country no less.

Lily watched Hailey walk away with Alessio and felt her anxiety surfacing once again. She took a few deep breaths and let them out slowly.

Padraig stood next to Lily and could feel her reticence. "Are you sure you are okay with spending some time with me, Lily? I know we just met but I want to get to know you better. Let's take a walk around the castle and enjoy the scenery. It's beautiful in my country, isn't it?"

Lily sighed, "Yes, it certainly is. I love it here. The countryside is breathtaking with all the green in every direction you look. It looks like someone made a gigantic quilt in different shades of green. It makes me want to make a quilt of my own to preserve it for myself when I get back home."

They walked along the grounds and stopped to view the ruins of the castle behind them. A spattering of drops began to fall and they hurried back to the mansion, Blarney House, to take refuge under a doorway. Padraig took off his jacket and put it around Lily's trembling shoulders over her own jacket as she smiled in thanks for this gentlemanly gesture.

As the rain came down harder now the couple looked off to the distance where the sun was now shining near the lake as a rainbow suddenly appeared in brilliant colors. Lily's breath caught as she watched it grow from one side of the lake to the other. She swore that she saw something race by toward the rainbow all in green with a pointy hat.

"Did you see that, Padraig? Something ran toward the end of the rainbow. Could it be? No, that's impossible!"

"My lady, nothing is impossible here in the Emerald Isle! I found you, didn't I?"

"Yes, I guess you are right. And I found you too! I feel as if I have known you forever, Padraig."

"Me too, Lily. I think we both found our end of the rainbow right here." These words were sealed with their first kiss, a magical one at that.

A little green man was smiling at the happy couple as he began to count his gold coins from the end of the rainbow.

THE END

PRINCE CHARMING

Sherry checked her reflection in the mirror one last time before heading out to work. She always did this to make sure her lipstick was on her lips and not on her teeth. The one time she didn't check was the time she met him. It was a day that had changed her life.

She remembered that day. She was rushing off to work, having slept in, which hadn't given her enough time to complete her morning ritual. She had brushed her hair in the car and hastily applied her favorite lipstick, pink rose, and raced off in her car.

She always stopped at the coffee shop near her office to pick up a large coffee, light cream, no sugar to start her day. Sherry was not a morning person and needed all the help she could get from the coffee. She stood in line tapping her foot and looking at her watch. Time was going by and the line still did not move. Sherry was about to leave the line and forget her coffee when someone tapped her on the shoulder. She turned around to see a man looking good enough to eat for breakfast. He had a three-piece suit, hair perfectly styled, and a wide grin on his handsome face. Sherry felt her heart pounding and her hands beginning to shake and for once in her life she couldn't talk.

"Oh, I'm sorry for startling you. But I see that you seem to be in a hurry. You can take my place at the front of the line if you want. My friend is saving it for me." He smiled an alarming smile with his perfect white teeth that hit her right between her solar plexus.

"Huh? Oh, I'm late for work already. Thank you. I will take you up on that offer." Sherry couldn't believe that she had found her voice. It felt like it was coming from someone else's lips.

The gorgeous man took Sherry's arm and led her to the front of the line where a man was standing staring at him with creased brows. "Well, Garner, it's about time. The girl already took my order and I was forced to order more just to keep her busy and keep your place in line."

"Okay, Freddie, don't worry. I am here with…" He looked at Sherry waiting for her to answer.

"Oh, yeah, umm, I'm Sherry. Nice to meet you Freddie and Garner." She sighed and was aware that Garner was still holding onto her arm.

The waitress harrumphed and cleared her throat to get their attention. "Can I help you?"

Garner ordered his latte and said, "For the lady please bring…"

Sherry finished his sentence with, "A large coffee, light cream, no sugar." And let out her breath that she hadn't realized she was holding.

Freddie leaned into Sherry and whispered, "You have lipstick on your teeth," before walking away with a satisfied grin.

"Oh my, oh no!" Sherry exclaimed as she grabbed her hot cup of coffee and ran out the door forgetting to pay for it.

When she got to her office she rushed in and pick up a mirror that she always kept in her top drawer and flipped it open. What she saw was disconcerting to say the least. There was lipstick across all her front teeth, pink rose. "Ugh, how awful," Sherry exclaimed as she pulled a tissue out of the box on her desk and made reparations.

She couldn't believe what she had done. Sherry messed up her chance to finally meet someone that she felt attracted to. *What would he think of her now?* She tried to get her mind back to her work before the new boss came in to see her. Sherry was a reporter for a local newspaper and was hoping to get bumped up to a higher position. She wanted to be the Department Head of Advertising for the paper.

She had her eyes on her computer and didn't notice the man as he opened her door and stood waiting for her to look up. "Excuse me, Sherry. Can you come to my office? I would like to speak with you."

Sherry tapped enter and looked up. She couldn't believe who was standing there - the man in the three-piece suit. "Oh my, I didn't know you were… umm, yes, of course."

Sherry followed the man out of her office to his own. She found her hands shaking once again and a pain in her chest from not breathing. *What was he doing here? Is he my new boss?*

"Please sit down, Sherry. It seems that I have startled you once again today. Not a good way to begin, is it?"

There goes the killer smile again. Sherry knew she was staring but couldn't help herself.

"Sherry, are you okay? Can I get you something, a glass of water maybe?"

"Yes, yes, please a glass of water would be great," she answered not knowing what else to say.

Garner, now her boss, pressed the intercom button for the secretary and requested a glass of water for Sherry.

Sherry turned to take the glass from the secretary but received another shock when she saw Freddie standing there. He winked and leaned in to whispered, "Looking good, Sherry."

She gave him a look that could have stopped snow from melting in the desert. She recovered and gave her attention back to her boss. *What was she to call him? She couldn't call him Garner?*

"I didn't expect to meet you in the coffee shop today. Sorry, I didn't realize that you worked for me. It's nice to see that you are dedicated to getting here on time. Hope you didn't burn yourself with the coffee when you left so suddenly."

"Oh, I'm fine, really. I'm sorry I rushed out before paying. Can I get you a cup of coffee later to make up for it?" Sherry couldn't believe what she had just said. It sounded like a pickup line. She cringed.

"Ha, that's fine. I may take you up on that later. Now let's get down to business, shall we?" Garner shuffled papers around on his desk and pulled out one to study.

"I have your file in front of me and your worksheet of accomplishments. Very impressive, Sherry, I must say. Do you still want to head the Advertising Department?"

Oh no, there goes that smile again. He is killing me with it. My mind has just gone blank! Sherry shook her head to clear it and looked off into the distance over her boss' head to avoid gazing into his blue eyes and that smile. "Yes, I do, Mr...."

"Garner Jacobson, you can call me Garner unless that makes you uncomfortable?"

"Well, I don't feel right calling you by your first name. I have never done that with a boss before, Mr. Jacobson."

"Okay, that's fine. It's probably better that you do that. It may look like I am favoring you over others for this position." The smile grew wider as his eyes began to bore into hers.

"Umm, well, I wouldn't want that. I think I have worked hard here and have done all that was expected and more on my position as reporter. I have been here for ten years now."

"Yes, I see you have. I think you would do a commendable job as Head of Advertising. Can you begin today?"

"Oh, yes, of course, I can! Thank you, Mr. Jacobson." Sherry jumped up and reached out her hand to shake her boss' hand. Mr. Jacobson stood up and took her hand and held onto it longer than was necessary as his eyes swallowed hers.

Sherry felt extremely uncomfortable as she pulled her hand free and backed away from her boss. She opened the door and walked briskly back to her office and once there collapsed in her chair. Something wasn't right about Mr. Jacobson. She now felt anxious being in his company. She didn't like the way he looked at her. He didn't even know her. *What was going on with him?* The feeling she had when she first met him had changed to cautious and uncomfortable.

There was a knock at her door and she looked up to see Freddie entering. She smiled at him relieved to see it wasn't Mr. Jacobson.

"Are you okay, Sherry? You look a little nervous. Did I scare you by coming in? I really didn't think I was that frightening to look at," Freddie chuckled.

"Oh, Freddie, I'm sorry. No, it's good to see you again. I was a little nervous about my meeting with Mr. Jacobson, that's all."

"I heard you got the job. Congratulations. That is the reason I stopped in, to tell you that you have a new office up on the third floor in the Advertising section. After all the boss has to be right there to keep an eye on things."

Freddie's smile was sweet and pleasant and not at all uncomfortable to look at. It gave Sherry a nice warm feeling in the pit of her stomach and she found herself responding with a smile of her own as she looked at him.

"Oh Freddie, what do you think of Mr. Jacobson? How long have you worked for him?" Sherry felt as if she needed to know more about this man that made her so anxious.

"What makes you think I work for him?" Freddie replied then settled down in a chair across from Sherry.

"Well, you brought in a glass of water for me and I thought you were Mr. Jacobson's secretary."

Sherry watched Freddie's face as he laughed heartily and his eyes sparkled in amusement. She waited until he composed himself for an explanation.

"Oh, I see. You thought...," he laughed some more before explaining, "No, not at all, in fact he works for me."

"What, you are the boss? I didn't know...oh I'm sorry, Freddie, I mean, Sir."

"Sherry, please call me Freddie. That is my name after all. I took over the business recently and wanted to observe the staff before announcing that I am the new boss. I have observed you and suggested that you be the new Head of Advertising. Garner is just doing a favor for me. He is my lawyer and quite a charmer and somewhat of a cad. Watch out for him."

"Wow, I didn't expect that at all. So, am I hired for the position?"

"Yes, my lady, you are. Relax and let's get you up to your new office. Oh, and by the way, you owe me for a coffee.

I paid for it, not Garner," Freddie laughed his contagious chuckle and smiled that wonderful sweet smile.

Sherry returned the smile and joined in with a laugh of her own. "I will repay you for that coffee, kind sir." She sighed in relief that this gentleman was her boss and felt comfortable in his presence. Sherry looked forward to working with Freddie and just maybe there could be something more for them in the future.

Freddie offered his arm to her and escorted her out the door. Sherry wore her smile all through the day and thought over everything that had happened. Sometimes a Prince Charming is found in unexpected ways, and there is such a thing as comfortably ever after.

THE END

A LAST GIFT

The town of Langster was a sleepy little town with less than 100 residents, some of which were related to those who had served in the Civil War. Everyone knew one another and Amber and her family always felt safe.

Amber walked along the side of the road until she came to her grandmother's house. Her mother had let her walk the short distance since Amber was nine years old. Grandma Alice requested that Amber stop by today for she had a surprise for Amber's sixteenth birthday which was the following day.

Grandma Alice was waiting in her favorite chair in the sitting room when Amber entered the little house. The sun was shining on her grandmother and she looked like a contented napping cat. Amber tiptoed into the sitting room and sat down next to her grandmother in the rocking chair that she had loved since she was a little toddler. Grandma Alice once promised this rocking chair to Amber when she got married and had a home of her own.

The creaking and rocking sound of the chair alerted Grandma Alice that Amber had arrived. "Oh, my dear, I didn't hear you come in. I did hear the creaking sounds when you rocked in your favorite chair. Have you been here long?"

"Oh no, Grandma Alice. I just arrived and made myself at home in this chair like I always do," Amber giggled like the little girl she once was.

The sound of Amber's laughter warmed Grandma Alice's heart. "It is so nice to hear your laughter, Amber. You are such a delight, dear child. I know that you are not a child but to me you will always be. You are special, you know that?" Grandma Alice cocked her head and smiled at her favorite grandchild. Though she had ten grandchildren, at the last count, Amber was always her favorite.

"Thank you, Grandma Alice. I don't feel special though. What do you mean?"

"Oh, I think you might know what I mean, dear child. Ever since you were a mere toddler you knew things long before what is considered normal. You were intuitive and seemed to know what people were thinking. Your anticipation of events was uncanny –you could predict things. When you were little you did not realize this ability. As you grew up you would tell me things that didn't happen yet. I have helped you hone your abilities. Have you had any more dreams about me or the family?"

"No…not really Grandma Alice. I sometimes dream about things but I don't believe they are real. Are they?"

"Well, that depends upon what you dreamed. Do you want to tell me about them? I promise not to share with anyone even your mother. You know that I never share what you say with anyone else. It has always been just you and me."

"Yes, I know and I trust you Grandma Alice. You have helped me many times over. I thought at times I was going crazy. My mother didn't understand what I sometimes said or felt. She dismissed my predictions as just an overactive imagination. I don't believe it was that at all. I thank God that I have you to believe in me."

"I think we need to thank God for all we have. We have been a fortunate family here in Langster. Not everyone has been as lucky as we, you know."

"Yes, I do, Grandma Alice. I wish I could have saved the Bishops when their house caught on fire." Amber couldn't go on for fear she would cry again. The Bishops lived at the end of the next street and had died in a house fire.

"It's not your fault, Amber dear. It was not your fault. You did save Nelson and his dog. It was tragic that his parents and grandfather didn't make it. But you couldn't have prevented that from happening. By the time the fire department arrived the whole house was up in flames. When you got there just before the fire department you only had time to alert Nelson and the dog who were in the kitchen about the fire. The others were upstairs in their beds and were already dead from smoke inhalation most likely. I am relieved that you didn't go into the house and try to rescue them too. You may not have made it out. I couldn't have dealt with losing you!"

"I did try to go back in but I couldn't get past the hall to the stairs. It was just lucky that Nelson was downstairs feeding the dog and having a snack of his own when the fire started. They think it was a fire that started in the dryer and crept through the walls."

"Now, let's talk about something more pleasant unless you want to tell me about your latest dream. If not, then I have something I want to give you for your birthday."

"Yes, I agree. Let's talk about something pleasant for a change. My birthday isn't until tomorrow, Grandma Alice. Aren't you coming over for cake then and to help celebrate?"

"I will, dear, but I wanted to share this with you alone. It makes it more special to do it this way."

Amber held back tears but nodded her consent. "Okay, I would love to have your present early, Grandma Alice." Amber had dreamt this was coming.

Grandma Alice reached over to the table next to her comfy padded chair and picked up a small box with a bow." She leaned forward to hand it to Amber with a smile that encompassed her whole face.

Amber took it from her grandmother and sat it on her lap as she looked at it a moment before opening it. Amber took off the bow and lifted the cover. What she saw brought tears to her eyes that brimmed and fell upon her lap. Sitting on the cotton was a gold locket. Amber picked it up and looked at it closely. There was writing on the back. *Good luck will always follow the one who wears this.*

"It's beautiful, Grandma Alice. I love it and will wear it every day."

"Thank you, dear. I knew you would. Now open it. I think this will be a surprise to you unless you saw this in your dreams."

Amber's hands were shaking as she opened the locket. Inside were two photos, one of Grandma Alice and Grandpa Charlie and the other of Amber's parents. Grandpa Charlie had passed away three years ago from a heart attack while on his daily walk to town. Amber's father had passed away two years ago, also from a heart attack but in his bed. Amber never got over the fact that she had lost them only a year apart. At the time of their deaths Amber had felt a sharp pain in her chest that could not be explained at the time.

"Oh, Grandma Alice this is so special to me. My two favorite men and you and Mom are here too! I will keep this close to my heart always. Does Mom know about this locket?"

"No, I didn't show it to her. I wanted to give it to you first. You can share it with her and anyone else you chose. It is truly special, Amber. It will keep you safe if you wear it every day. Nothing bad will ever happen to you. I may not be here much longer to protect you."

Amber's eyes widened at what her grandmother just shared about herself. "Oh, Grandma you will live a long time yet. Please don't talk like that. I need you in my life. What would I do without you?" Amber's tears flowed as she covered her face with a tissue. She refused to believe her recent dream.

"Amber, please don't cry. We all have to leave this world some time. I will always be with you here." Grandma Alice placed her hand over Amber's heart.

Amber held onto her grandmother's cold hand and took it in hers to warm. She kissed it and patted it and smiled up at her grandmother. "Yes, I promise I will wear it daily and know that you are with me always."

"Now child, it is time for me to take a nap. I am so tired. This old body is slowing down and needs to be recharged. I wanted to make a cup of tea for you. Sorry the time went by so quickly and now I am too tired to do it." Grandma Alice yawned and settled comfortably laying her head against the padded back.

"I can make you a cup of tea, Grandma Alice." Amber looked over at Grandma Alice and noticed she was already sleeping peacefully.

Amber leaned down to kiss the soft cheek of her grandmother and got an afghan off the back of the couch and placed it over her grandmother to keep her from getting chilled.

She backed away and closed the door quietly and headed back to her mother's house. Her mother, Maureen, was baking a cake for her birthday and looked up when she saw Amber. A welcoming smile reached her eyes before her lips and she beckoned Amber forward. "How was your grandmother doing? Is she coming over tomorrow for your birthday?"

"Yes, she said she would but I will go over to get her. She will insist on walking over alone if I don't. She gave me my present early, Mom. Do you want to see it?"

"Of course, dear. Give me a minute to get this cake into the oven. I made chocolate and will frost with dark chocolate frosting. Okay? I know you love chocolate, honey."

"Thanks, Mom!"

Amber touched the cool smooth surface of her locket and opened it to admire the photos once again.

"Ooh, is that what Grandma Alice gave you? It's beautiful, Amber. I never saw that before. She must have hidden it away all this time waiting for you to grow up and be old enough to appreciate it. Oh my, is that a picture of your dad and me? That was the day of our wedding. I never saw this photo of your grandmother before. It looks like it was at their wedding too. Grandma Alice never showed this to me. I wonder why?"

"I don't know Mom. She didn't tell me. Did you see what it says on the back?"

"No, let me see." Maureen turned the locket over and read the inscription. "I wonder why she put this on it. Does she think you are in danger? Your grandmother was always psychic. I think you seem to take after her too. I have never had any premonitions and I'm glad of that. It's too creepy to know something is going to happen before it does."

Amber suddenly looked up and saw a flame shooting up out of the oven. She grabbed her mother and pushed her forward out of the kitchen as the flame appeared to follow them as it raced up the wall and across the kitchen.

Amber heard her grandmother's voice calling, "Get out of the house now."

Amber and her mother raced out into the yard and turned around as the house went up with a bang. The gas stove exploded and flew up out of the roof landing on the sidewalk several feet in front of them.

"Oh my God, what happened?" Maureen exclaimed as she hugged herself in alarm.

"I don't know, Mom. But if I hadn't heard Grandma Alice's voice I may not have moved fast enough to save us."

"You heard Grandma's voice? I didn't hear her."

"I heard her in here," Amber explained as she pointed to her head, "and here too," she continued pointing to her heart.

"I guess your grandmother was right. Wearing this locket that connected you to her may have saved our lives." Maureen enveloped Amber in a tight hug as they both shook from the near-death experience.

Two houses down from Amber's, Grandma Alice opened her eyes and smiled in relief knowing she had saved her daughter and granddaughter. She closed her eyes again for the last time.

Amber felt the loss at the same time and held onto her mother tighter as she cried tears of both sorrow and relief.

THE END

THE CLOWN

The door opened silently but there was no one there. Kent closed his eyes tight not wanting to see the ghosts or goblins waiting for him. He had asked his father to close his closet door and put a chair in front of it. His father promised he would do that and also leave a night light on. But now the door was opened and the night light was off. He shivered underneath his covers and tried to calm his racing heart.

There was a noise. What was that? He opened his eyes once again and looked around in the dark recesses of his room. He couldn't see anything. He started to say his prayers to God to keep him safe from the horrors of this night. Suddenly there was a creaking sound next to his toy box. His rocking chair was moving. Was there something sitting on it?

Kent couldn't believe this was happening. He knew it was Halloween tomorrow. Maybe someone is playing a trick on me, he thought. There are no such things as ghosts, goblins, and things that go bump in the night. He kept repeating this to himself until finally he fell asleep.

The next morning he sat up in bed and rubbed his tired eyes and looked around. What he saw made his gasp in shock. Sitting in his rocking chair was a large stuffed clown. He slid out of bed and stealthily moved over to get a closer look. Yep, it was a clown and its eyes were closed. He poked and prodded it and then picked it up. Where did it come from? Did his parents want to surprise him with a stuffed clown for Halloween? He hated clowns.

He tucked it under his arm and headed downstairs to ask his parents. They weren't there and neither was his sister. He went back upstairs and peeked into his parent's bedroom. Their bed was made. Then he checked his sister, Jen's room. Her bed was made, which was unusual. She never made her bed unless threatened by their mother. Where was everyone?

The clown was getting heavy as he walked back to his room. Something was wrong here. He put the clown back onto the rocking chair and slipped back into bed. Before he closed his eyes once again he looked over at the clown. Its eyes were now wide open. He screamed!

"Kent, wake up! You are having a nightmare. It's okay. Mom is here."

"Oh, Mom. It was awful. There was a clown and his eyes were opened and you and Dad and Jen were not in the house. I was so frightened."

"What clown dear? You don't have a clown. You always said you hate clowns."

Kent looked over at his rocking chair which was now empty. He jumped out of bed and looked under the bed and into the closet which was barred by a chair. There was no clown.

"Oh, I must have been dreaming. Is it time to get up yet, Mom?"

"Yes, dear. It's time. I'll make you some pancakes with blueberries. Okay? That should make you forget about your dream."

"Thanks, Mom!"

Kent pulled out his clothes and started getting dressed. As he picked out a pair of socks he noticed something at the back of his drawer. It was the clown! He screamed and ran out of his room.

"Kent what is wrong? Why are you screaming? You aren't having a dream, honey. You are awake," his mother yelled up to him.

When Kent went downstairs his mother was nowhere in sight. The house was still. When he turned around the clown was waiting for him at the foot of stairs.

THE END

CALISTA ROSE

Calista Rose sat on her favorite tulip as she thought over what she was going to do. She didn't like being sad all the time and decided to do something about it. The other fairies were all busy doing whatever they needed to do each day while she never seemed to have anything to do.

Early in the morning, when the dew was still fresh on the lawns and flowers, Calista Rose took her purple pouch and headed out to explore and find something to keep her busy, and thus, make her a happy fairy. She flittered from flower to flower collecting the sweetest nectar and depositing it into her pouch where she had compartments for all kinds of things. She also picked her favorite flower petals and sealed them in another section for use later.

Calista Rose was so busy that she found herself humming a song that she hadn't hummed since her mother taught her as a baby. She found that she was feeling light and airy and happy! Calista Rose moved swiftly through the currents of air as the sun rose and shined down on the grass and flowers making them sparkle like gemstones as the sunlight caught the dew.

She looked down on the village that spread in front of her, noticing it for the first time. Her mother had warned her many times to stay away from the village. The humans there did not understand about fairies, and if they captured her, they would try to make her use her magic in evil ways. These humans were not all evil but her mother wanted to keep her from venturing too far to find out.

Calista Rose fluttered up to a tree that was hanging over a sweet little cottage that looked like it was made out of candy and flower petals. She had to get a closer look and touch it to see if it was. Just as Calista Rose placed her index finger on the roof of the cottage she heard a voice.

"What are you doing to my roof? If you touch it, you must give me my wish."

The little fairy jumped back in alarm and looked around as she flew back up into the nearest tree. There was nothing around and no one in sight. Who was talking to her?

Calista Rose edged forward once again and extended her finger to touch the roof. The voice grew louder and angrier as it said, "What are you doing to my roof? You now must give me my wish."

"I'm sorry. I didn't mean anything by touching your roof. I was curious, that's all. It looks like candy and flower petals. It smells like them too," Calista Rose explained.

"Who are you, and what are you doing here?"

"I am Calista Rose and I wanted to do something to keep busy like all the other fairies. I didn't realize I had come so far though."

Out of the front door of the little cottage came a little girl in a tattered dress and no shoes. She had long blonde hair and large green eyes. Her curls bounced as she walked. She looked up at the fairy in the tree and smiled. The little girl put out her hand and beckoned the fairy to come closer.

Calista Rose couldn't help feeling curious and moved closer and landed in the palm of the little girl's open hand. She settled down and crossed her legs as she raised her hand and waved at the child and smiled her best smile.

The little girl laughed in delight and waved back to the fairy. "Hi, Calista Rose. It's nice to meet you. I am Sonya Leia and I am five years old. How old are you?"

Calista Rose thought over what she was going to say. "I am older than this village and you together."

"Can you really do magic and make my wishes come true?"

"Yes, of course, Sonya Leia. Was that your voice I heard when I touched your roof? It sure didn't sound like you."

"Oh no, it was the roof talking. It doesn't like to be touched," Sonya Leia giggled once she saw the confusion on the fairy's face.

"What did you say?" Calista Rose asked quite perplexed.

"Oh, sorry, it was my father. He is blind and thought you were a witch."

"Oh my, me a witch? Never, never could I be a witch. I am just a little fairy and will never do you or your father any harm."

"That's okay, Calista Rose. I told my daddy I would go outside and see what was on the roof and shoo it away."

Calista Rose looked at the little girl standing in front of her and noticed her tattered dress and no shoes upon her feet. She looked a little pale and thin too. Mustn't be getting enough to eat, she thought.

"What would you like to wish for, Sonya Leia?"

"Oh, there is one thing I have wished for since I could talk."

"Yes, yes, what is it?" Calista Rose was anxious to know.

"Well, my daddy is all the family I have. My mommy died having my brother and he died too, shortly afterwards. I want my daddy to have his sight back. He lost it in an accident and now can't work. I have to help him cook and clean the house and lead him around. He says that I am his eyes." Sonya Leia bowed her head as a tear dropped from her eye.

"Oh, dear me, of course little one, you have your wish granted. Go inside your house and greet your father."

Sonya Leia ran into her house and laughter could be heard as the fairy turned to go back home. Before she could get up into the tree once again Sonya Leia ran out and called her. "Calista Rose, thank you so much for making my daddy see again! He is so happy and so am I! Oh, and thank for the new dress and shoes too. I love blue; it's my favorite color."

"You are welcome my new little friend. Well, I must go now before it gets dark or I will not find my way home." Calista Rose waved goodbye as the Sonya Leia waved backed and went into her house. More exclamations of joys could be heard as Calista Rose flew home. She had waved her hands over the village and granted everyone's wishes and stocked their cabinets with enough food to last the whole year.

As Calista Rose neared her home all the fairies were out and about flittering around and looking anxious. The King Fairy, Quentin, flew over to Calista Rose and scolded her. "Where have you been, Calista Rose? We have all been worried sick about you. You never venture very far from home but today you were not in any of the usual places. Where did you go?"

"I'm sorry but I didn't realize how far I had gone until I got to the village."

"The village you say? You are never to go to the village!"

"I know, but I met a little girl and…"

"Never, never go near the village, Calista Rose! It is filled with evil beings! You could have been kidnapped or killed. Many fairies have ventured into the village and have never returned." King Fairy Quentin shook his head as he flew back to his castle.

"Oh my!" Calista Rose smiled and felt truly happy even after the warning as she thought over what she had done and her new little friend. She knew that Sonya Leia was not evil and that the village was filled with good humans.

Back in the village Sonya Leia smiled happily as she ate her fill and admired her new blue dress. Her father sat next to her and patted her hand and said, "Good job Sonya Leia, for tricking that fairy into giving us wishes. We will not need to ask for anything more until our food runs out once again."

He looked over at the cages holding several fairies. They no longer were colorful and had lost their magic. He needed a new one. He would wait for the little fairy to come back. They always did. Then he would make his move.

THE END

THE DREAM

She woke up in a sweat and looked around. It was her bedroom and nothing seemed to have changed. Why was she afraid? What was she afraid of? She tried not to go back to sleep for she feared being chased. Her eyes closed against her will and it all began again.

She was traveling in a dark passage of a large Victorian house. The only light was at the end of the corridor, a gas light on the wall that flickered and danced around. It caused shadows to appear and disappear except for one that stayed in place. She slowed her progress when she spied it. The shadow was elongated and reached the darkness beyond the light. Did it just move toward her? She felt goosebumps on her arms and the hair on the back of her neck tingled. She turned and began to run. She ran faster than she had ever run before in her life. Her life might just depend on her speed. She turned her head to look behind her. What she saw was incomprehensible and she screamed!

The shadow followed her closely and stopped when it realized that the human was frightened after the woman screamed. All the shadow wanted to do was talk to the woman. She didn't want to hurt her. The shadow had been trapped inside this house for centuries and wanted to be released from its prison.

The shadow reached out a black hand and touched the woman on the arm. After the woman screamed she fainted and fell to the floor. The shadow leaned over to look at the fallen woman but could do nothing to help. It waited until the woman awoke and tried once again to convey its problem to her.

The woman sat up and screamed once again when she saw the shadow standing over her. The shadow made a whispering sound as it placed its black finger against the woman's lips. The woman shook from fright and was frozen in place with the shadow's finger resting on her lips. What was surprising was the coolness the woman felt and suddenly she was calm. She listened to the whispers and nodded to the shadow. The shadow reached out its hand to the woman and the woman took it. The shadow gripped the woman's hand and both were lifted upward. A light appeared at the end of the corridor, but this was not from the gas light on the wall. It became brighter and burst forward catching the shadow and the woman as they both floated in the air. The woman could feel the shadow releasing her hand as the shadow quickly disappeared and the woman floated back down to the floor.

The woman woke up and felt a calmness this time. She looked around her bedroom to assure that she was alone. The sun was coming up and the room was brightening. She went over to the window and opened the blinds to let in more light to chase away any shadows left.

She had moved into this Victorian house a few days ago, inheriting it from her great, great grandmother. She was the last of the family and all alone in the world. She went out into the corridor, the same one that was in her dream. She turned on all the lights, electricity not gas lights. There against the wall was an outline of a shadow and on the face was a smile. She touched the face and felt a coolness that dissipated quickly. She turned to get away from this phenomenon and then looked back but it was gone. She heard a whisper, "Thank you, Faith, for releasing me."

Faith was her name but who and what was that? Could it be her great, great grandmother? She shook her head and continued toward the kitchen to make a cup of tea. In the tea canister was a letter. Faith opened it carefully, for it looked as if it had been there a long time. She spread it out on the table and sat down to read.

If you are reading this, you must be a relative of mine. My name is Faith and I have been locked inside this house since the day I died. No one has ventured forth to help me. If you can please release me from this prison. I cannot leave until you help me. Only a relative of mine can do this. Once you release me, the house will be free of spirits. I have stayed behind to keep the evil spirits at bay. They will harm you.

Faith couldn't believe this but she knew what had happened in her dream. She had released her great, great grandmother who now could Rest in Peace. Faith looked down at the paper and noticed another line of writing that suddenly appeared.

Thank you, Faith, dear child, for releasing me from my prison. All I needed was a touch of your hand and the spell would be gone. Now you are safe from the evil that dwelled here. I was killed by my lover and left here for eternity. He will get his due, for now I am free.

THE END

THE WELL

The land was verdant and lush with plenty of fruit trees, elm, maple and oak trees that spread far and wide over thirty acres of land. The old farm house was in ruins now. No one had lived here for fifty years. The place was thought to be haunted. No real estate agent would touch it. It was thought to be a lost property.

In its heyday, the farm was thriving and successful. Horses roamed the land, chickens clucked their way around the barnyard, and vegetables and fruits, plentiful from the land, kept the family fed through the long winter months. Life was perfect until the second well was discovered.

The farmer and his dog were exploring the northern part of his property and stumbled upon a second well. It had been partially covered with overgrown shrubs and high grass. The farmer moved away the overgrowth and looked down the well. He threw pebbles into it to check for water and depth. There didn't seem to be any water and the depth was not conclusive. He couldn't hear the pebble reaching bottom. He called his dog and headed back home to tell his wife about his find. He planned to return early the next day to explore it further.

After discussing his find with his wife, the farmer prepared to set off early the next morning with rope, flashlight and his trusty dog to explore the well. His wife warned him to be careful and not spend too much time exploring for there was much to be done on the farm. The farmer promised and hurried on his way.

The farmer tied a rope to the nearest sturdy tree and threw the rope into the well. He clipped his flashlight to his belt and turned it on to light his way. He began his climb down stopping to feel the sides of the rocks and examine the walls more closely. He still could not see a bottom. As he got closer to the end of his rope he stopped and looked down. What he saw astounded him. He reached his foot out and kicked what looked like a bone. In fact there were multiple bones hanging from the sides of the well. He raised his flashlight to view this spectacle and cried out in alarm. The bones were not only animals but humans too. The bones were piled up along the sides of the well and reached down as far as his light would go. There must have been hundreds of bodies here. How did they get here and why?

He felt his body shaking from the dampness and cold that seemed to be intensifying as he climbed downward. He suddenly heard voices coming from below him. How could that be? They beckoned him to join them. He quickly grabbed the rope and began to climb upward at a much faster clip than before. All he wanted to do was get away and never come back to this graveyard. He was almost at the top when his dog began to bark loudly.

The next moment was a blur as his dog catapulted down into the well and disappeared. The farmer cried out and looked down moving his light back and forth in an effort to find his dog but to no avail. He was gone forever, swallowed up by this monstrosity of a well. The farmer's tears ran freely as he grieved for his dog and pulled himself up the last two feet and out of the well. He couldn't tell his wife about this. What would he tell her – the well took his dog? She would think he was crazy. He did feel like this was only a dream and that he would wake up and find his dog alive and well.

The farmer pulled up the rope and looked down the well once more but there was no sign of his trusty dog. He trudged home and went back to the barn to complete his chores until it was time for lunch. His wife placed a large bowl of stew in front of him, but he had lost his appetite. He avoided looking at his wife as he tried to eat a little.

"What's wrong dear? Where's Rusty?"

The farmer stuffed his mouth so that he couldn't answer and kept his head down. He mumbled with a full mouth and kept eating. He felt nauseated.

His wife shrugged her shoulders and went back to finishing up her lunch and cleared the table. She kept her eye on her husband because she knew something was terribly wrong. He wouldn't look at her and was not enjoying his lunch. That was not like him at all. He always asked for seconds. He had barely eaten half of his stew and now had left the table. She vowed to go look for Rusty on her own and find that well he mentioned.

The farmer's wife grabbed a flashlight, snuck out of the kitchen and went in the direction her husband had taken earlier that morning. She walked for fifteen minutes until she noticed branches and grass that had been pulled out and scattered around. She kneeled down and turned on her flashlight over a dark area in front of her. It was the well. She moved the light over the well's sides and in the center as she tried to see the bottom. She heard something faint coming from the well. It sounded like voices and a dog barking.

"Rusty, is that you? Where are you boy?" Her voice echoed and was swallowed by more voices begging her to join them. They increased in volume and intensity. The farmer's wife stood up and turned to get away but found her foot trapped by a root. It pulled her and knocked her down. She gripped the roots and grass around the well and tried to pull herself up. But something below her was pulling her down. The voices were getting louder as the pull on her body became stronger. She screamed. As she was falling into the well she cried out one last time, "God help me, please!"

The farmer finished feeding all the livestock and bedded them for the night. He felt ashamed that he hadn't spoken to his wife about what had happened to the dog and vowed to make amends. He entered the kitchen which was spotless with no sign of his wife. That was strange. She always started supper early and called him in to get cleaned up. She really must be upset with me, he thought.

He called out to her in their five-room house without any luck and went outside to search for her. He walked in the direction of the well. He thought he heard her voice calling him. "Where are you dear? I'm coming," he replied. The farmer ran forward and stopped right next to the well. He could hear his wife calling him and his dog, Rusty, barking. He reached down with his flashlight, looked into darkness, and called out to them. The next minute he felt a strong pull, but as he tried to back away he lost footing and fell head first into the well.

Many years later the farmhouse was sold to another family. The young family couldn't believe their luck to find this beautiful lot for such a low price. The couple had been out driving around the area when something seemed to draw them to the property. They went into town and found a realtor to assist them.

The realtor mumbled something about ghosts but the couple was so enthralled with this property that they didn't pay much attention to the realtor. They were happy to finally have a place of their own for their three children.

The house needed repairs and the young man immediately began repairing the current five rooms and then adding on an addition of three bedrooms and another bathroom. The three boys were bored helping their dad day after day and decided to go exploring one morning. Their mother warned them to be careful and come back for lunch. They nodded in agreement and ran off in a northerly direction.

THE END

ONE WISH

Tara Lynn sat on the bench that bordered the pond, the same pond she often visited with her parents when she was a little girl. She loved watching the lily pads floating along in the water and the frogs jumping from one pad to another. She had always giggled when she saw a frog snatch an unsuspecting insect with its tongue as the insect flew too close to the lily pads. She wished she was a little girl now, she sighed.

"Why was I in such a hurry to grow up? Now I am grown, married and with an apartment of my own to clean." She looked at a frog who was sitting on a lily pad. He appeared to wink at her and listen. "I have a husband who…" she choked on the next words, "who is demanding, assertive and stubborn about everything I do. I feel like I am in prison. He doesn't let me breathe. Being here with you, little frog, is the most peace I have felt all day."

She looked down at her watch. "Oh, I must leave or I will not have time to finish up cleaning and cooking before Gary gets home. Bye little frog. See you again soon, I hope." She bowed to the frog and waved. Out of the corner of Tara Lynn's eye there was a movement from the frog. *Did he just wave back at me? Oh boy, I am really losing it now!*

Tara Lynn jumped into her car and took off as quickly and safely as she could. Luckily, she only lived a couple of miles away from the pond. She looked forward to the next time she could visit her favorite place.

There were some good times she remembered when she and Gary had first met and during the time he courted her. They were both sixteen and still in high school. He was cute with curly blond hair and blue eyes. He had come to her parents' house to sell some magazines. Her father had invited Gary in and offered him a drink and talked the poor boy's ear off before buying the magazines and letting him escape.

Tara Lynn watched Gary interact with her father and felt smitten and he was too, she found out later. Things went quickly from there. They went to her prom together but Gary had already invited another girl to his prom before he had met Tara Lynn. That didn't make Tara Lynn very happy to say the least. But Gary soon broke off with the other girl and he and Tara Lynn went steady from then on.

Gary went into the Army right after graduation and was in the service for four years.

They had a few spats while he was overseas about what Tara Lynn was wearing in one of the photos she had sent him. She attributed it to Gary being homesick but he was also jealous of her going out with friends. Tara Lynn had sewn her own mini skirt; at that time, they were the rage. She thought it was perfect but Gary did not. They almost broke up over that argument but his father, good man that he was, talked Tara Lynn into staying with Gary.

During one of his leaves Gary had arranged to have enough time off for them to plan their wedding. It was a beautiful wedding and Tara Lynn was happy until Gary told her that they would have to move away a month after they wed to Utah for ten months to finish off serving his time.

Tara Lynn was extremely close to her family and they all found this difficult to separate for that long a time. Tara Lynn's brother, Tim, was six years younger than she while her sister Molly, was fifteen years younger. Molly had a traumatic time getting used to Tara Lynn being away for so long. Tara Lynn was like Molly's second mother.

While Tara Lynn and Gary were in Utah, he had played mind games with her. He tormented Tara Lynn in psychological ways by telling her she was nothing, stupid, couldn't do anything right, etc. Tara Lynn cried mountains of tears day and night and prayed constantly that she would be freed from this treatment. If this was love, then she didn't want it. Gary told her he loved her but didn't show it by his actions and unkindness.

Tara Lynn wasn't allowed to call her parents from Utah because Gary said they couldn't afford the telephone charges so Tara Lynn wrote copious letters. She always loved writing and honed her abilities during those long, exhausting and miserable ten months. They should have been deliriously happy being newlyweds. Tara Lynn questioned whether she had made a mistake in marrying Gary and wondered where the loving guy was that she thought she knew. Maybe he wasn't showing his true colors back then, she thought.

One day Tara Lynn begged Gary to let her get a dog for company. Gary was away all day on base and she was alone and miserable. Tara Lynn couldn't find a job due to being a wife of a serviceman and having a temporary living situation. Gary consented only because he loved animals more than humans. They went to a nearby kennel and chose a little dog, eight pounds and full of adorableness, a mixture of two different terriers. Her name was Rosie and she became Tara Lynn's savior.

Tara Lynn lavished Rosie with all the love she was holding inside and soon Tara Lynn could see the light at the end of the proverbial tunnel. Before Rosie had come along Tara Lynn was despondent and was contemplating suicide as a means to escape.

Time finally came for them to move back home. Tara Lynn couldn't get ready fast enough. The Army sent over a crew to pack up their dishes, household stuff while Tara Lynn took care of some of her personal things. These men were really something to watch in motion. They even packed up all their clothes. These men moved with precision like the soldiers they were. *Wish I could have them each time I move. Oh no, that would mean Gary would have to be a lifer! No! Couldn't handle that!* Tara Lynn thought out loud.

Well, they all survived somewhat but Tara Lynn was a changed person when she came back home to Massachusetts. Gary had broken her spirit and it would take a long time to repair.

Now that they were settled in a little apartment back in their old home town, Tara Lynn hoped things would get better. Less than a week after they arrived back home Gary had started in on Tara Lynn about how she washed their clothes. In his mind a dryer was not needed unless it rained. This meant he expected her to line dry all their clothes all year round, even in the dead of winter.

She found a position as a secretary in a local business and had to work a full-time job. Gary expected her to continue to do everything in the house, cooking, cleaning, washing and drying on the line. All this was getting to her. She was young but even the young get tired especially when a person has to come home and put out clothes in the dark and the next morning bang the ice off of them when they freeze over. Tara Lynn started wearing mittens to do this chore.

Tara Lynn's mother, Elaine, called her daily to make sure Tara Lynn was doing well. She knew Tara Lynn was depressed and knew why from the little her daughter had told her in the many letters she received during those ten months away. Elaine Withers would cry after reading each letter and then show her husband, Frank. He would just shake his head and his voice would take on a serious tone as he said, "Listen Elaine, we cannot interfere. Tara Lynn must take care of this situation herself. She married him.

She must love him. If we interfere she will hate us in the end. The decision is hers. If she needs us she will ask. You know I will do anything for her. You must be patient, my dear."

"Oh Frank, I know, but I feel so helpless." Elaine cried more tears as she went back to cooking dinner to calm her nerves.

***

What the Withers didn't know yet was the fight Tara Lynn and Gary were then having over Sunday dinner. Tara Lynn cried out, "Gary stop it right now. I want my parents to come over for dinner next Sunday. Why are you being so hard to get along with? I love my parents and haven't seen them much since we came back except for a few minutes here and there. You always seem to have an excuse not to go over to their house and now you are doing the same thing when I want them to come here. I need to see them; don't you understand that?"

"No, I don't. My parents don't come here and I don't want them here anyway. They are not needy and clingy like yours are. If I want to see them I just go over there myself."

"My parents aren't needy and clingy. They miss me. After all we were away for ten months, Gary! Why are you like this? Why do you torment me? Every time I want to do something you give me a hard time." Tara Lynn put down her fork and began to clear the table. She had lost her appetite.

"Where the hell do you think you are going, Tara Lynn? I did not finish my dinner and neither did you! Get back in here now!" Gary's face was beet red and he clenched his fists on the table and spoke as he gritted his teeth.

Tara Lynn knew this was a warning and a serious one at that. She knew it wouldn't take him long to get up from the table and punch her right in the face. He had pushed her a few times and said he was sorry but the look on his face those times showed anything but regret.

Tara Lynn returned to the table and sat down as Gary finished his dinner and left the table for her to clean. She tried to keep the tears at bay but she was so unhappy. Rosie was at her side as soon as Gary left the room. The poor dog was afraid of him too. She was Tara Lynn's dog through and through and would follow her anywhere.

When Tara Lynn went to the pond she would leave Rosie home, for the dog would get into all kinds of muck running around the pond. Tara Lynn feared that Rosie would leave some telltale signs of the muck somewhere in the house. Then Gary would know about her place of solitude. She couldn't give that up to him.

She cleaned the dishes, washing them all instead of putting then into the dishwasher. Heaven forbid if she did that. According to Gary it was laziness to use it at all. Tara Lynn couldn't figure out why he even wanted to buy it. She never got to use it unless they had company and they never had company.

Gary had so many quirks that Tara Lynn didn't know how she hadn't seen some of this weird personality before. One thing that drove her nuts was when he insisted she only use three sheets of toilet paper each time she used the bathroom. He was definitely insane when he would check to see how long it took her to use a roll. Tara Lynn started hiding the little rolls and replacing them with a new one each time. She secretly bought more toilet paper and kept replacing the small rolls with what she had in the closet.

Another weird thing was regarding Sunday breakfast. Gary insisted Tara Lynn make a full breakfast including baked beans, sausages or bacon, scrambled eggs, toast, coffee and orange juice. The one time that she forgot to buy baked beans Gary went into a frenzy throwing things around the house and screaming obscenities at Tara Lynn. She learned not to forget any of the items for Sunday breakfast from then on just to keep peace.

The other days of the week Gary requested two eggs sunny side up and she better not break the eggs or there would be hell to pay. Tara Lynn would always be a wreck when she had to cook them and inevitably ruined many eggs over the year before getting them Gary perfect.

Going to work each day was a release for Tara Lynn from all the insanity at home. She got out of the house and met people and interacted with both men and woman. Gary never took her out to dinner or a movie unless she begged or promised him something in return which was usually sex. She dreaded that now too. She was beginning to hate him more and more.

Tara Lynn started to dream about ways to kill Gary. She prayed right after these thoughts to God for forgiveness. She knew she wasn't capable of doing that, but sometimes Gary pushed her too far. She felt despondent and didn't know where to turn. Most of her friends had fallen by the wayside because of his attitude toward them. Even her parents and siblings were nervous around him and avoided coming as often as they would have liked. She was alone and forgotten and would have to take matters into her own hands.

The next day at work she made a list of ways to get back at Gary and teach him a lesson. He was nothing but a bully and a bully would back down if only she could be more forceful. She had to work on it.

Her boss dropped in unexpectedly as she was typing her list. He came up behind her and cleared his throat to get her attention. "Tara Lynn, sorry to interrupt your work. Looks like you are pretty busy typing away like that. Do I work you that hard?" Dylan Andrews quickly read over her shoulder as he waited for Tara Lynn to answer.

Tara Lynn jumped up in alarm. "Oh, Mr. Andrews, I am so sorry I didn't hear you come in. I was just catching up on some stuff." Tara Lynn avoided meeting her boss' eyes.

She didn't see Mr. Andrews' concerned expression once he realized, from what he read, that this woman was in trouble. He smiled to put her at ease as he said, "No problem Tara Lynn. You're a good worker and always doing more than your share. Take a break now. I was just coming in to say that I didn't have anything urgent for you to take care of at present." Mr. Andrews smiled at Tara Lynn and patted her on the arm to get her to move. She was just staring at him with her mouth open.

"Oh okay, thank you, Mr. Andrews. I guess I could use a cup of coffee." Tara Lynn printed out her list and tucked it into her pocket before leaving her office. She smiled at her boss as she grabbed her coffee cup and headed down to the break room.

Oh my God. I hope he didn't see what I was typing. He would fire me for sure and think that I am deranged or something. I'm beginning to think I just may be insane.

Tara Lynn pulled out her list and read it through.

1. *Stab him in the middle of the night as a warning (I couldn't do this!)*
2. *Put poison in his food or drink (No!)*
3. *Tamper with his brakes on his car (I don't know how to do that.)*
4. *Run away and never come back (Take Rosie with me!)*

5. *Stand up to him and tell him to go to Hell! (Ha ha!)*
6. *Demand a divorce (Most likely)*

Tara Lynn sipped the rest of her coffee and left the break room. She peeked into her office but there was no sign of her boss. She settled down at her desk and got to work after putting her list into her pocketbook for later.

The day ended too quickly for Tara Lynn. She dreaded seeing her husband each night. He was never in a good mood and soured her mood too. She recited the list that was now in her head. Which one should she use first?

When Tara Lynn arrived home, she put Rosie out quickly. She watched Rosie do her business and urged her to come right back in. There were wild creatures out in the woods that could be a danger to a little dog. Tara Lynn fed Rosie and added fresh water to her bowl and gave her a loving pat and hug before going back out to get the frozen clothes.

Wearing warm gloves helped her to easily bang the ice off the clothes as she took them off the line and placed them into the basket. Once she got back into the house she started folding them and putting them away. One of her husband's underwear was still caked with ice but instead of taking it off she placed it into his drawer between other underwear. Her husband would have a surprise when he took them out in the morning. Let him complain; she was fighting back now.

The dinner that night was his favorite, beef stew. In his dish she added some laxatives and mixed them up with extra gravy and meat. He never noticed anything different and asked for seconds. She happily obliged.

In the middle of the night she put his slippers far away from his side of the bed while he was sleeping. Tara Lynn knew how crazy he got if he did not have his slippers nearby to slip his feet into. He didn't like walking around without them. He would get a surprise when he got up and couldn't find them.

The next morning there was a lot of yelling and hollering as Gary jumped out of bed and couldn't find his slippers. He then had to race to the bathroom because of the effects of the laxatives. When it came time to dress Gary pulled out his underwear that was damp and angrily searched through his drawers for a dry one.

While all this was happening Tara Lynn was down in the kitchen making breakfast and then hurrying out the door to work. She didn't want to stay around to be the brunt of his wraith. She couldn't help giggling all the way to work over what she had done to him. Well, it served him right for being such a bully.

At work she reviewed her list and vowed to contact a lawyer to begin proceedings for a divorce. After the lawyer heard what she had been through with Gary the lawyer would gladly file papers swiftly. Her only concern was that she could be in danger because of Gary's anger.

She told her parents what she planned to do leaving out what she had done that morning and they gladly offered her old room to stay in as long as she needed. Tara Lynn arrived home earlier than Gary and packed her clothes into two suitcases along with personal items and looked around for anything else she would need. She picked up Rosie, her bed, food, and toys and stood by the door as the tears rained down. She couldn't believe that this was happening after a year of marriage.

She hurried out the door to her car as Gary was driving up. She put the car in reverse and flew out of the parking space as he looked at her with pure hatred on his beet red face.

Tara Lynn arrived at her parents' house and they greeted her with open arms and hugs. Rosie was excited to see them too. She loved them and felt this love reciprocated. Tara Lynn sat down at the table with her parents over coffee and cake and explained everything. They were shocked over the horrendous treatment their daughter had to endure and agreed that seeing a lawyer would be the best avenue to take.

Frank Withers called his friend who was a lawyer to set up a meeting for Tara Lynn. He explained a little about what Tara Lynn had been dealing with for a year. The lawyer agreed to see her that night in his office.

Tara Lynn was anxious about having to relive the craziness during her short marriage. But once she began her story it flooded out along with a mountain of tears as the lawyer, Samuel Thorenson, listened, nodding and taking notes. When Tara Lynn had exhausted all the details and answered Atty. Thorenson's questions she felt a profound relief settling over her. She no longer had a headache and her shoulders relaxed. Tara Lynn felt light-hearted for the first time in a year.

Atty. Thorenson looked up from his notes and smiled. Well, Tara Lynn, it looks like you have grounds for a divorce. I will set things in motion and call you to come in and sign all the necessary papers. I think it was a good idea to get out of the house and stay somewhere safe. If Gary tries to come near you or threatens to harm you, please let me know right away. I can get a restraining order on him. In the meantime, stay away from your apartment. If you need to get anything out of it, please call me and I will go along with you.

"Thank you, Counselor. I appreciate your time and assistance. All I want is to get out of this marriage and begin a new life free of fear and retribution."

Back at the apartment Gary was destroying everything of Tara Lynn's that he could. He had already trashed her closet and knickknacks in the living room. The neighbors next door called the police when they heard all the noise.

When the police arrived, Gary had settled down and made excuses that he couldn't find something and had knocked over a few things in the process of looking. The police asked if they could come into the house and look around. Gary stepped back reluctantly for them to pass. As they looked around they noted that it was much more than Gary was stating. They would report to their supervisor and proceed from there.

Gary swore and called Tara Lynn every name in the book. He grabbed a bottle of Jack Daniels, a box of cheese crackers for dinner, and settled down in front of the TV. He vowed to get back at Tara Lynn and make her pay for what she had done to him that morning. No woman was going to get away with making a fool out of him, he thought.

Tara Lynn took Rosie for a walk that weekend to her favorite place of all, the pond. She sat down and put Rosie on her lap where she snuggled close and promptly fell asleep. Tara Lynn thought back to the past few days and how much better she was feeling being away from Gary. She had heard from the police about his destruction of their apartment and Atty. Thorenson suggested a restraining order. She didn't feel right about it and begged the lawyer to wait a little on it. Tara Lynn knew this would only anger Gary more. She wanted to wait until he calmed down and came to his senses, if that was at all possible. She sighed as she watched the frogs hopping from lily pad to lily pad and snatching the insects out of the air.

The divorce would not be legal for several months yet and Gary was giving the lawyer a hard time about signing the forms. He claimed that he loved Tara Lynn and couldn't live without her. This, she knew, was not the case. He would soon find himself another victim to trap and imprison.

She had been staying at her parents' now for a few months while she saved all the money she could from her pay after giving her parents some for rent. They did not want to take it but she knew that they were living on their pension and meager social security checks. She did all she could to help them out by cooking, cleaning and shopping. It would be hard on them when she moved out at the end of the month.

Atty. Thorenson obtained a decent settlement for her and she did not lose anything that Gary had destroyed. Gary was forced to repay Tara Lynn for everything that he had damaged. He would think twice about doing something like that again. They would have to split their bills and moneys once the divorce was final.

Tara Lynn had found an apartment close to work which would be perfect. On good days, she could even walk there. Her boss had been kind to her during this time and offered to help her in any way he could. He was a good man and appeared more than just interested in helping her. She let him know in a good way that she was not ready for another relationship. Her divorce would be final in a few months. Tara Lynn just wanted to find herself and begin again fresh without depending upon anyone else but herself. She felt like she was being reborn.

Tara Lynn now laughed as she used as much toilet paper as she wanted, put all her dirty dishes into the dishwasher and dried all her clothes in the dryer. Her one wish - to be happy - had finally come true!

THE END

HAROLD'S PLAN

It just has to work! If it doesn't, what am I going to do? I don't want to live a life without love. Harold thought. He couldn't take it anymore. No one looked at him and no one seemed to care.

Harold was not handsome by any means but he was conscientious about his appearance. Harold did what he could with what little he had by keeping his brown hair neat and clothes clean and pressed. His best feature was his deep brown eyes that were expressive especially when he was happy, which unfortunately wasn't often.

He had been in love with this girl, Francesca, since high school. She was always friendly to him but never showed any interest in him as a boyfriend. Harold thought Francesca was beautiful with her long flowing blonde hair that he dreamed of running his fingers through. Her blue eyes were stunning, and he found he could not stop looking at them. Harold considered her an angel. She was a little shy and didn't get many dates because of that. He was relieved that she didn't date often because he wanted her all for himself.

Harold had been at the top of his class in both high school and college and finished his doctorate a few years early. He knew everything there was to know about computers. He had started a business to design his own line of computers and programs. He had been busy putting together the newest line of computer games and came across an unusual sequence. This sequence would put the player inside the game. The only catch was that they must not let go of the red button while the game was running or they would be stuck inside the game forever. Only he knew how to get out of the game.

He wanted to impress Francesca with this new game. He called her and asked, "Hi Francesca. How are you? Do you want to come over to my office and see my newest computer game? We could split a pizza and have some colas." Harold waited for her response.

"Oh, I don't know if I can right now, Harold. My car is at the mechanics. That's great that you have a new game. You are an expert at this stuff. I don't use the computer very often unless I have a paper due. Maybe we can do it another time."

Francesca was about to hang up when Harold responded sadly, "Okay, but I can come over to your house instead if that makes it easier for you. I'll bring a pizza and colas over in a jiffy." A dial tone was heard and Francesca put down the phone and shook her head. *I should have told him 'no' more firmly. He is such a nice young man but I am not interested in him that way.*

Harold ran out the door grabbing the game pack with the special button attached. He went to his favorite pizza place and ordered a pepperoni pizza and a liter of diet cola. He knew that was what Francesca drank. Harold was shaking with excitement and drove a little too fast to get to her house. He had a couple near misses as he screeched around the corners.

Francesca was waiting at the front door as Harold came out of his car with the pizza, cola and game pack. He smiled up at her and his heart skipped a beat or two as he entered her house. Francesca smiled but not with her eyes. She was just going through the motions. She knew she had to tell Harold today before he tried to ask her the question again about being his girlfriend.

"Hi Harold. Nice to see you. So, what do you have to show me? I think you are on your way to being famous. Maybe even more famous than other programmers."

"Well, I don't know about that but I do know that I have something that no one else has right now. I wanted to share it with you first before I show the world." Harold beamed at her and reached out to touch her hand.

Francesca reacted by moving away to put the pizza on the table with plates, forks and glasses. Harold noticed the slight but didn't show his emotions. He sat at the table and they ate in silence for a few moments until he began to explain, "Francesca, I am excited to show you this program. It is incredible. It can do amazing things. In fact, I can't just talk about it. I want you to try it. I have been the only one to try it out and I need your opinion of it. It will blow your mind! But first let's finish our pizza and colas. I got your favorite pizza and diet cola. Did you notice?" Harold sat back and smiled at her.

"Umm, yes, I see you did. You are very thoughtful and kind Harold. Thank you. I...need to talk to you about..."

Harold pushed away from the table, pulled the game pack out of his jacket and went over to Francesca's computer. He set up the game for Francesca to try. He pushed away from the desk and put out his hand in invitation to her.

Francesca took a quick swallow of her cola and walked over to join Harold at her computer. He quickly gave her the instructions on how to proceed with the game and repeated how important it was that she hold onto the red button and not let go during the game unless he told her to.

Francesca frowned and agreed to do exactly as Harold had instructed her. The game was going well and Francesca seemed to be enjoying herself as she traveled through several layers of the world. With Harold's help, she managed to make it to the end where she was at a castle covered in gold. Her eyes opened wider as she entered the castle and saw everything she had always wanted – jewels, clothes and her favorite foods.

Francesca was fascinated by this room in the castle and turned to ask Harold about it. She noticed, though, that he was no longer by her side at the computer but inside the game. She was so flustered that she took her hand off the red button and the next moment she appeared next to Harold in the castle.

"What just happened?" Francesca screamed!"

"Nothing, my dear, but you did take your finger off the button. Now we can be together for all eternity!"

The buzzing of the computer game ended snuffing out the tormented screams of Francesca.

THE END

REAL MAGIC

Eric always loved magic. When he was just three, his father taught him how to make a coin disappear. Well, not really disappear, but you know, hide it behind your back and then magically make it reappear behind someone's ear.

Eric thought that was the best trick ever. From then on, he was hooked on magic and on each of his birthdays he asked for more books on magic and kits to practice on. Eric envisioned himself to be another Houdini one day. His skills grew exponentially and after he was out of college he got a chance to entertain as a magician in a local playhouse.

The crowds at first were minimal only including Eric's close friends and some neighbors and of course his parents and siblings. He said silent prayers that he could come up with a new exciting trick or illusion and become successful.

Eric had two brothers and one sister who always supported him in his endeavors. There was some jealousy at first amongst the brothers but that soon diminished when Eric included his brothers, Mike and Jerry, in all his tricks. There were two years between each of the brothers. His sister, Julie, being the youngest, came along ten years after Eric, wasn't interested at all and kept her distance when the boys were practicing. She feared that they would make her disappear and not be able to bring her back. The boys had tried but she was too quick for them to catch and always went into her hiding place, the back of her closet.

The night before the big show at the local playhouse, which was a full house, the three young men practiced a new trick with a crystal ball. It would involve picking a young lady from the audience to take part. Eric was nervous about this trick. He had not performed anything like this before and wasn't quite sure about it. He pushed his brothers to help him perfect the trick in order to allay his anxiety.

Julie poked her head into Eric's dressing room. "Hey Eric, how are you doing? Are you sure about this trick? You seem to be a little nervous. You are never nervous. What gives?" Julie sat down on the battered couch that was pushed against the wall and partly covered with all kinds of paraphernalia.

"Hi Sis. I'm…well, I guess I have my nerves under control now. It's just that I haven't done this trick before. I want to attract the audience's attention and I have to have new material all the time. I don't want them to get bored looking at the same tricks night after night."

"Oh Eric, I don't think they will. You are fantastic. I can't believe you do what you do sometimes. I can't figure out any of your tricks even when I watch them closely."

"Thanks, Sis," Eric laughed at his sister's naiveté and at the same time felt humbled by her confidence in him.

"I'm sure you will knock it out of the park or should I say the theater?" Julie smiled and her whole face lit up as she looked at her brother with admiration. He was always her favorite brother. He was the one to take time to play with her when she was young even when he was busy with school and work.

"I will be cheering you on, Eric. Bring it, Bro!" Julie chuckled, blew him a kiss and left the room.

Eric ran the trick through his head for the twentieth time, so it seemed, before feeling better about it. Mike and Jerry came in and high-fived their older brother before sitting down on the couch.

"Well, are we all set, Eric?" Mike queried, anxious to begin the show.

"Yeah, I guess I am," Eric sighed.

"What? Do you mean you are not sure of it yet?" Jerry asked with a shaky voice.

"Oh, no, I'm okay with it now. I went over a few things in my head before you came in. It will work, don't worry. If I'm not worried you shouldn't be either." Eric tried to sound positive.

The venue manager, John DeMarco, knocked on the door and stuck his head in to announce, "Eight minutes till show time, fellows. Are you about ready?"

"Yes, Mr. DeMarco, we'll be ready," Eric replied warily.

Two minutes before show time Mr. DeMarco knocked on the dressing room door again and announced, "Show time, gentlemen."

The three brothers jumped up and headed out of the room and lined up behind Eric as they prepared to go onstage when announced. The lights went up and the applause began as Mr. DeMarco stepped onto the stage with a mike in his hand. "Welcome everyone! This is quite a crowd tonight. You are in for a treat. Let's get on with the show! Here is Eric Wolf and Company."

The applause began again and continued for a few minutes more as Eric and his brothers came on stage. They took their places, Eric at front and center and his brothers on each side of him in the back.

Eric swung his black and silver cape up over his head and around his body to make an opening statement. It looked impressive he knew. Oohs and aahs could be heard from the audience.

Several tricks and illusions later the audience was energized and ready for the big one. Eric could feel their excitement and anticipation as he began to explain what he would be doing next.

"Now, I have an illusion or trick or whatever you might think this is. It is something I have never done before. Not even Houdini has done this one. It involves a crystal ball, a female volunteer and some magic. The crystal ball is going to project the outcome of the trick in front of you. We will be projecting the crystal ball onto the screen overhead so you can see it up close."

Eric moved forward and once again swung his shimmery silver and black cape over his head and around his body up and down and around a few more times for effect. He motioned to his brothers to bring in the table with the crystal ball and place it in the center of the stage in front of him. Mike and Jerry carried the table and laid out a black tablecloth over it and then placed the white crystal ball in the center as the audience watched in awe and held their breaths in anticipation.

Eric stepped closer to the crystal ball and waved his hands over it and silently prayed that this would work. He turned toward the audience and raised up his hands as he said, "Now I will need the help of one young lady. Who is brave enough to come forward?"

No one moved, and a hush went over the audience as many looked around to see if there were any volunteers raising their hands. Eric was disconcerted until suddenly a young woman with long golden hair stood up and walked toward the stage. Her hair glistened as if it were on fire and there was a golden aura around her that was as brilliant as a rainbow after a storm.

Eric held his breath as this vision came closer. He reached down to take her hand and assist her up onto the steps to the stage. Eric felt his breath coming quicker as her hand warmed his cold one. There was a tingling sensation as she got closer and their eyes met. Something was different about this woman. She smiled a smile that was not of this world for it encompassed her eyes and her whole aura. Eric looked around to see if everyone else was seeing what he was. But no one seemed to be effected in any visible way.

Mike and Jerry observed their brother's odd behavior with this woman and cleared their voices to get his attention. Eric's head jerked upward away from the woman and toward the noise behind him. Mike mouthed, "What are you doing? Get going!" Jerry held the mike up for Eric to get his attention.

Eric grabbed the mike from Jerry and began, "Thank you for offering to come up here. You are a brave soul. What is your name?" Eric tried to keep his voice from shaking as he felt a tingling going through his whole body. He couldn't stop from shaking all over. He only hoped this wasn't evident to the audience.

"Hi, Mr. Wolf. It's nice to meet you. My name is Anastasia."

"Well, nice to meet you too, Anastasia." Eric took her hand in his again and shook it lightly feeling a stronger tingling traveling up his arm and hitting him between the eyes. He swayed slightly but he felt Anastasia holding onto him as he righted himself.

Eric shook his head to clear it and looked around. His brothers were shaking their heads and whispering, "What's wrong, Eric? Start the illusion!"

"Let's begin, shall we?" Eric led Anastasia toward the table. He motioned for Mike to bring over a chair to the table. Mike had to go backstage to find one. This wasn't part of the illusion.

Once the chair was situated at the table Anastasia sat down and waited for further instructions from Eric. All the time she kept a beatific smile on her face.

"Anastasia, we are going to make you appear inside the crystal ball. First, I will use my cape and raise it in front of you. After some magic words, you will appear inside the ball. Are you ready?"

"Yes!" Anastasia exclaimed clearly excited about the concept.

Mike and Jerry stepped forward to assist holding the cape in front of Anastasia as Eric waved his hands over Anastasia's head and whispered his words of magic. The brothers dropped the cape on cue and the chair where Anastasia sat was now empty.

The audience screamed and applauded wildly and stood to demonstrate their enthusiasm for the surprise performance. All eyes went to the screen above that showed the crystal ball and Anastasia inside it.

Eric and his brothers gasped when they saw the ball. Not only was Anastasia inside the ball but the crystal ball was now floating in the air above the table.

The audience kept applauding and hooting and hollering as the ball moved around the stage on its own accord. Eric tried to put his hands up to catch it but it moved away from him. His eyes locked with Anastasia's inside the ball and she smiled and nodded as the ball came down into Eric's hands and he brought it back to the table.

Mike and Jerry were speechless and exchanged startled looks with one another as they quickly moved closer to the table waiting for their brother to signal the next step. They couldn't believe what they were seeing. This, also, was not part of the illusion.

Eric took his cape and swung it up and around the crystal ball to complete the illusion and bring Anastasia back. As he brought it over his head he felt lighter as if he were floating. What happened next was the unexpected. The next moment Eric disappeared from the stage and appeared inside the crystal ball next to Anastasia.

Mike and Jerry stood transfixed and didn't know what to do next. They looked at the crystal ball again and noticed that it was now empty. Standing in front of the table stood Eric and Anastasia holding hands.

The audience was stunned and a hush could be heard as the reappearance of Eric and Anastasia registered. Then a cacophony of a startled audience began.

Eric raised his hands and took a bow as he kept a hold of Anastasia's hand the entire time. She took a bow along with him and then disappeared down the stairs and back to her seat.

When the audience left the theater Mike and Jerry along with Julie and their parents met Eric back stage. They expressed their joy over his outstanding performance. "Eric, you were incredible! How did you ever do that? Where is that young woman?"

"I really don't have any idea how that happened. I didn't do it! I am as surprised as you are. I don't know where the woman is. She disappeared after the performance."

Word traveled far and wide about the incredible illusion. It was now making the local venue too small at 525 capacity. Soon Eric would have to look for a larger place to perform. Eric did not see the woman again until he was at his next venue and began the crystal ball illusion. At this time she would appear from the audience and perform the trick with Eric and then disappear.

Eric was now famous and was known all over the world for this fantastic illusion. He was distraught and wanted to find the woman, but the only time he saw her was when he performed the illusion.

Over the years many magicians and illusionists tried to get Eric to give away the secret of how he performed this illusion to no avail. He knew that it wasn't his doing but Anastasia's, for her name meant – resurrection.

THE END

THE TRUE MEANING OF CHRISTMAS

Chapter 1

The little girl's name is Clarinda. She is ten years old with long dark brown hair and beautiful blue eyes. She can't remember what it's like to be warm or to have a full stomach. It's two days before Christmas and the house is bare of any signs of the holiday.

Clarinda woke up this morning and heard someone crying. She got up, grabbed her thin bathrobe and wrapped it around her quickly as she tiptoed over to the door. The floor felt cold under her feet and she felt around for her slippers, tattered as they were, they would be better than nothing at all to keep her feet warm. As she slowly opened her bedroom door the sounds were louder and she realized that they were coming from her mother's room.

Clarinda's mother, Miranda, was not well and hadn't been for as long as she could remember. Her mother had progressively gotten weaker since her last two pregnancies with Clarinda's siblings, Andrew, four and Brenda, two. Clarinda listened as she passed by her sibling's bedroom to make sure they were not awake and needing her attention before going to her mother's room.

In order to put food on the table for the family, Miranda had to take in washing and ironing for well-to-do people. They paid well enough for her to keep her children in mended clothes and provide some meat on the table at least once a week. Her husband, Holden, had died in a tragic car accident shortly after their daughter, Brenda, was born, leaving Miranda penniless, with three children to care for.

Miranda sat on the edge of her bed with her head in her hands as she cried. Her mind was whirling since the loss of her husband and she was devastated that she was too weak to continue working to take care of her children. She couldn't afford to buy food, never mind Christmas presents. Miranda looked up as the door to her bedroom slowly opened and Clarinda's head popped in.

"Mommy, are you okay? Why are you crying?" Clarinda's beautiful blue eyes looked at her mother with surprise and concern. They belayed her age and showed a deep intelligence. Clarinda's eyes mirrored her father's and only broke her mother's heart more each time she looked at her. The other two children favored their mother with their green eyes and blond hair.

"Oh, sweetie, I'm all right. Just a little tired today. Don't worry, everything will be fine. Can you be a good girl now and go check on your brother and sister and bring them down to breakfast. I'll make your favorite today – pancakes. We have one egg left and enough flour to make a few pancakes. You have been such a big help to Mommy. Now go on. Hurry up, honey."

Clarinda left her mother's room and went to check on her siblings. Andrew and Brenda shared the same room and both were awake and chattering together as Clarinda entered. She told Andrew to get dressed after she selected his clothes and changed her sister's training diaper and dressed her in her pink pants and top. Brenda always wanted to wear pink – it was her favorite color. She smiled her sweet toddler smile after she was dressed and cuddled with Clarinda to say "thank you."

Clarinda loved her brother and sister as if they were her own children; after all, she had been both a sister and a mother to them since they were born. She did all she could to help her mother but she was only ten and didn't realize a lot about life yet and what it entailed to raise a family. She closed her eyes, took a deep breath, and took Andrew and Brenda by the hands and brought them down to the kitchen for breakfast. The enticing smell of pancakes was in the air and she found herself salivating and hurrying to set the table so they could eat. Their dinner the night before had been meager with a potato and a little gravy made from a soup bone and a piece of bread to sop up the precious liquid.

She put Brenda in her high chair and told Andrew to sit down as their mother flipped the first pancakes onto their plates. Clarinda had to cut up the pancake for Brenda and blow on the pieces so she wouldn't burn herself trying to eat too fast. Brenda made 'num num' sounds as she stuffed the pieces into her mouth as fast as she could. Clarinda took care of her siblings first before taking her first bite and felt herself melting with the delicious taste.

Miranda looked over at her children as they ate like it was their last meal. But, she thought sadly, it could be if her health didn't improve soon. She didn't know what she was going to do. She didn't have anyone to turn to and didn't want to lose her children if she asked the state for help. Clarinda was such a godsend and was already doing so much to help her. Could she ask her to do the washing and ironing too? No, she thought, she would have to do it herself but have Clarinda bring the basket of clothes to the Antonelli's house and receive payment. Yes, that is what she would do.

Clarinda cleaned up the children's faces and then tackled the table and the dishes in the sink as she waved at her mother to go lie down and rest. Miranda kissed her sweet daughter's face and patted her on the head as she passed by to go to her room to rest.

Miranda called out to her daughter on her way to her room, "Thank you, sweetie, for cleaning up. I will just rest a little and then I will tackle the clothes and ironing. If you could bring the clothes over to the Antonelli's afterwards and pick up the payment that would be a great help to me."

"Of course, Mommy, I will be happy to help you. I will watch the kids while you rest. I love you, Mommy." Clarinda was fearful that her mother was going to die like her father did. She told her mother every chance she got that she loved her, thinking that maybe she would keep her healthy longer that way. She always felt terrible that her father died before she could say, "I love you, Daddy," one more time. Clarinda could feel tears brimming in her eyes and used her sleeve to wipe them away so that her siblings wouldn't see her crying. She had to be strong for them.

Miranda lay down and fell asleep as soon as her head hit the pillow. She stirred in her sleep dreaming of her husband and his hand was reaching out to her. She reached forward in her sleep to touch his hand but it was too far out of reach.

Chapter 2

While her mother slept, Clarinda kept the children busy as she read several books to them. At least they had books that she managed to get from the library that were going to be thrown away. They were tattered just like the rest of the things in her life.

It was nearly noon and her mother still had not woken up. She would have to feed the children their lunch and then tackle the clothes. Clarinda knew that if she didn't get the clothes over to the Antonelli's today they would not get paid full price for the wash. She put together the last two slices of bread to make a bread and butter sandwich and split it between the children. While they were busy eating she would start the wash.

There was a small basket in the laundry area which was filled with their clothes and the larger basket was the Antonelli's. Clarinda put in the first load and added the detergent which was getting low. She made sure to use it sparingly so she would have enough to finish all the clothes. While the machine was going she hurried back to check on her brother and sister. Andrew and Brenda were just finishing up the last of their sandwiches and looking for more. Clarinda checked the cabinets once again for anything to fill their little stomachs before her own. She found a few crackers which she doled out to them and ate one herself. That would be the only lunch she would have. She wasn't a large person. However, she felt she could afford to lose weight but not her younger siblings who needed the nourishment more. She gave them each a full glass of water to fill them up more before putting them both down for a nap. After tucking them into their beds she hurried back to the clothes to transfer the clean ones to the dryer and the dirty ones into the washer. At this rate it would take all day to finish washing the clothes besides having to iron them too.

Clarinda worked tirelessly for two hours without stopping until she heard Brenda crying. She rushed through the last bit of ironing and shut off the iron. As she headed into the children's room she was greeted by smiles and happy jumping as Brenda put her arms out to her from her crib and Andrew got out of bed and snuggled close to her side. Clarinda wrapped them both in her arms and held them tightly wanting only to protect and keep them safe – if only she could. She was getting concerned about her mother since she still hadn't awakened.

With the children by her side she guided them to their mother's room to see if she was ready to get up now. Clarinda needed for her mother to watch the children while she took the clothes to the Antonelli's.

When she opened the bedroom door she noticed her mother's arm was hanging over the side of the bed. She moved closer and turned on the light on the night stand. What she saw made her cry out in alarm. Her mother was still and not breathing. Clarinda shook her mother's shoulder and called out to her. Clarinda was afraid that her mother might be gone and never wake up again. The children started to cry as they felt something was wrong when Clarinda cried out and only clung tighter to their sister.

Clarinda picked up the phone on the night stand and called Dr. Harvey who was their family physician. When his secretary, Denise, answered, Clarinda couldn't speak. Tears kept flooding her eyes and chocking up her speech. The children only cried louder making it even more difficult for Clarinda to hear Denise as she asked what was wrong. Denise waved at Dr. Harvey as he came into the office and pointed to the phone mouthing that it was Clarinda. He picked up the extension and asked, "Clarinda, what's wrong sweetheart?" Dr. Harvey yelled into the phone to try to be heard over all the crying. "Where is your mother, dear?"

"Sss....she's in bed, Dr. Harvey. She's not moving and I can't wake her up. I don't know what to do. I have to take the clothes to the Antonelli's or Mommy will be angry and she won't get paid. Can you come over and help me?" Clarinda sniffled and wiped her eyes and nose on her sleeves as she tried to hold onto the children at the same time. They were so frightened they wouldn't let go of her anyway.

"Of course, Clarinda, I will be right over. Just sit tight and I'll come and check on your mother and stay with the children while you take over the clothes. Okay, dear? Please don't cry now. I'll be right there." Dr. Harvey put down the phone. His hands were shaking as he took in what the poor child must be dealing with. He needed to get over to her house immediately. Dr. Harvey was an old fashioned doctor who at one time did house calls. He had known Miranda since she was a child herself.

Dr. Harvey instructed his secretary to hold all calls and postpone his afternoon appointments and that he would not be in the office the rest of the day. Denise nodded sadly, "Of course, Dr. Harvey. Is there anything I can do?"

"No, Denise, but thank you. I need to find out if Miranda is okay and find someone to stay with the young ones. Clarinda is in such a state over the Antonelli's clothes. I didn't realize how bad things had gotten for the family. I feel terrible that I could have helped the Davis' in some way and didn't. Could you please lock up after you contact all the patients? Go home early, Denise, you work too hard and need a break. Thank you for everything."

"No problem, Dr. Harvey. I hope Mrs. Davis is okay. If you need a babysitter I can go over there after I leave here. Call me on my cell. Okay?"

"That is very kind of you, Denise, but I think I can manage. But it is good to know that you are available in case I need you. Thank you. I will see you tomorrow."

Dr. Harvey left his office and waved at some arriving patients who looked a little concerned that he was going out when they were coming in. All he could think about was what he would find when he got to the Davis' house.

Clarinda paced back and forth with Brenda in her arms and Andrew hanging onto her right leg. She kept looking out the window hoping to see Dr. Harvey's car. It had only be twenty minutes since she spoke to him. He did say he was coming. But she was worried because her mother still hadn't awakened.

Dr. Harvey pulled into the Davis' drive and got out of his car. He looked up and saw Clarinda in the window waving at him to come in. He could see she was still crying and the children were upset too. He carried his medical bag with him as he stepped up to the door. He didn't get to knock as the door was pulled open and Clarinda ran into his arms choking back more tears.

Dr. Harvey patted her on the back and held her as she cried uncontrollably. He moved into the living room with Clarinda hanging onto him while the little ones hung onto her. He wanted to console her but needed to get into Miranda's room to check her out. He was concerned that she was close to comatose if what Clarinda said was true about not being able to wake her up. He only hoped he wasn't too late to help her.

Chapter 3

"Clarinda, please sit down and try to calm yourself so the little ones won't be upset too. Okay, dear. I will go check on your mother and be right back. Why don't you give the children something to eat while I am gone?

"We....we don't have any more food, Dr. Harvey. I gave the children the rest of the food for lunch. That is why I have to go to the Antonelli's to get paid for washing and ironing their clothes." Clarinda started crying again and this time couldn't stop. Her siblings started whining and fussing once they saw their sister upset again.

"Oh, my goodness, Clarinda, I am so sorry I didn't know. I will take you over to the Antonelli's, child, and then we will all go out to get something to eat. Okay? Now just sit tight and calm the children down."

Dr. Harvey sadly shook his head and felt a deep guilt for not knowing how bad the situation was for this poor family. He vowed to get them some help as soon as he assessed the medical health of their mother.

Dr. Harvey opened the door to Miranda's room and flicked on the light. What he saw wasn't good. Miranda was laying on her side with her left arm hanging over the side of the bed. Her eyes were closed and he couldn't detect any movement in her chest to indicate she was breathing. He pulled out his stethoscope and bent over her body to listen to her lungs and pulses. Her chest was congested and he detected a light heart rhythm and he lifted up her eyelids to check her pupils which were reacting to light. She would need to be hospitalized with what appeared to be a severe case of pneumonia. Dr. Harvey lifted up the phone and called the hospital to get an ambulance for Miranda ASAP.

His next concern was to take care of the children. Dr. Harvey obtained the Antonelli's number from Clarinda who kept it on the refrigerator. He made another call to the Antonelli's on the next block to see what they could do to help. Dr. Harvey knew of the Antonelli's and their affluence. If anyone could help it would be them. He was aware that they did not have any children of their own.

"Hello, yes, this is Mrs. Antonelli. Who is this?"

"This is Dr. Harvey. I am with Miranda Davis and her children. I need your help, Mrs. Antonelli. I learned from

Clarinda, her ten-year-old daughter, that she was to bring over your wash and be paid for this service. Is that correct?"

"Oh, yes, but Mrs. Davis always brought over the wash not her daughter. What can I do for you, Dr. Harvey? I don't understand."

"Well, Mrs. Davis is very ill and is going into the hospital and will be unable to take care of her three children. If I call social services Mrs. Davis could lose her children to the system. Do you think you could help her by taking her children in until she is out of the hospital and well enough to take care of them again? I really don't know where to turn at this time. They are really in desperate need and it is almost Christmas. Do you think you can help?" Dr. Harvey waited what seemed like minutes but were actually only several seconds before Mrs. Antonelli uttered a word.

"I see. I didn't realize that Mrs. Davis was sick or I wouldn't have asked her to continue to work for me. I am sorry to hear that. I also didn't realize she had three children. I only know of Clarinda. How old are the other two children?" Mrs. Antonelli's voice sounded a little surprised by the fact that there were three children to care for.

Dr. Harvey continued to persuade Mrs. Antonelli as he said, "Besides Clarinda who is ten, there are her brother Andrew, four, and sister, Brenda, two. Life has not been easy for them and Clarinda has been taking care of them all by herself since her mother has been sick. Anything you can do to help would be greatly appreciated. I need to take Miranda to the hospital now so if you could come over here and watch the children or pick them up and take them to your house it would be helpful. Oh, and Mrs. Antonelli, please feed them. They haven't had much to eat today." Dr. Harvey was getting a little anxious for Mrs. Antonelli's answer as he watched the ambulance pull up outside the house.

Mrs. Antonelli finally answered positively, much to the relief of Dr. Harvey, "I will be right over to pick up the children, Doctor."

"Thank you, Mrs. Antonelli. I appreciate your help. It will mean a lot to Mrs. Davis too. She is in a bad way right now and can't thank you herself but I will let her know what you are doing as soon as she is lucid. Merry Christmas, Mrs. Antonelli."

Mrs. Antonelli answered back, "Merry Christmas, Dr. Harvey." But the phone in her hand was sounding a dial tone.

Chapter 4

Mrs. Antonelli, Angela, as most people knew her, grabbed her coat off the high coat rack and her keys off the counter and went out to the garage to her Bentley to drive over to Mrs. Davis' to pick up the children. She was not a cold person but was anxious about having to take care of three children. She never could have any of her own though she and her husband had tried for many years until she knew it was not to be. She didn't know if she could do this but to refuse would be inhumane since Mrs. Davis was going to the hospital and had no one to take care of the children. She would just have to do her best and soon their mother would be back in good health.

Angela pulled into the drive next to the ambulance and ran up to the door as the EMTs rolled out a stretcher with Mrs. Davis. She moved aside and went into the house and was met by Dr. Harvey. Behind him stood three little waifs who looked scared, lost and so sad. She noticed they had all been recently crying which touched her deeply. She wanted to wrap her arms around them and tell them it was going to be all right. But she found that she couldn't move and didn't until Dr. Harvey brought her out of her stupor.

"Mrs. Antonelli, please come in. Let me introduce you to the children - Clarinda, Andrew, and Brenda. They have been looking forward to meeting you and staying with you until their mother is well."

Dr. Harvey leaned forward and whispered out of earshot of the children, "Thank you, Mrs. Antonelli. It means the world to me and to Mrs. Davis. Clarinda will pack up some clothes and things for herself and her siblings and be ready to leave shortly. Now I need to follow the ambulance and get to the hospital to take care of Mrs. Davis. Thank you again, Mrs. Antonelli. It is wonderful of you to do this. I will contact you to see how the children are doing in a day or so," turning back to the children Dr. Harvey said, "Take care children and be good for Mrs. Antonelli."

Mrs. Antonelli turned to look at Clarinda but was at a loss for words as she watched the tears flowing from the ten-year-olds' eyes. It hurt her deeply to see the child in such torment. Angela offered Clarinda her handkerchief to wipe her tears and watched as the child composed herself and put on a strong front for her siblings who looked on with frightened faces. They were just babies, thought Angela. What was she taking on? Could she do this?

Angela waved at the little ones and put her hands out to them and they came forward and grabbed onto her fingers.

They were visibly trembling from everything going on around them. Angela could see they were confused and frightened and missed their mother. She waited at the door with the children holding tightly to her fingers as Clarinda came back with her hands full of clothes and a few ragged stuffed animals. She rummaged around in the kitchen for a plastic bag in which to put their clothes and stuffed animals.

Chapter 5

Now it was time to go to Mrs. Antonelli's house. Clarinda really didn't know anything about this lady but what her mother had told her - she was a cold woman who didn't like children and never had any of her own. Would she be good to her and her siblings? She would protect her brother and sister and not let this lady hurt them in any way. She took a deep breath as she always had to get her strength up and face whatever was ahead. She turned to face Mrs. Antonelli who was holding onto her brother and sister.

Mrs. Antonelli looked kindly at Clarinda and said, "Hi Clarinda, it is nice to finally meet you. Your mother mentioned you to me. I hope you and your brother and sister will be happy staying with me while your mother recuperates. Do you have everything you need? If not, I will get whatever you need for all of you. Don't worry about anything, dear. Let me take care of you." Angela waited to see what Clarinda would say but she just looked at Mrs. Antonelli with eyes full of tears threatening to fall.

Mrs. Antonelli beckoned for Clarinda to come forward so they could leave. The children were getting antsy and tired and were hungry. They hadn't eaten since noon time.

Clarinda only hoped that Mrs. Antonelli would feed the children so they would be able to sleep the night through with full tummies. She couldn't remember, since her father died, when she last had a full tummy at bedtime or any time.

Angela led the children out to her car after locking up the house and making sure that Clarinda had a key to get back in, in case she forgot something. After making sure the children were snapped into seat belts with Clarinda holding onto her Brenda, she headed home. She would have to make sure she purchased car seats for the younger children. At least she didn't have to go too far with them since she only lived a block away and didn't have to worry about being stopped and fined for not having them in car seats.

When they arrived at her house, Angela went to the kitchen and began preparing a nourishing dinner for the children. They looked a little pale and underfed and by what Dr. Harvey said they were very needy. Looking around the room at their house she hadn't seen any signs of toys that children always leave out and about. She reminded herself to make a list for toys and more snacks that kids like for her next shopping trip. The saddest of all was the lack of any Christmas decorations for the children

in their house. She would take care of that, too, before
Christmas.

Chapter 6

In the meantime, Angela had a lot to do and for once in her life felt alive and full of purpose and needed. Her husband was expected from work shortly and she would call ahead to prepare him for what she had promised to do.

Leonard was a kind man and would be more than accepting of their three young visitors. He had made his millions selling video games online being a computer guru. They had started out with nothing, but once his first game sold, it took off and money started rolling in. Angela never had to work from then on. They had bought this huge house with the intention of filling it with children but it was not to be.

Angela dialed her husband and Leonard answered in his usual gregarious voice, "Hi Doll Face! How are you? You couldn't wait for me to come home – you missed me that much? Is everything okay, love?"

"Yes, sweetheart, I just wanted to tell you something that I did today. It's very important and I needed to help and…" Angela didn't know how to tell him but finally blurted it out, "I took in Mrs. Davis' three children; the lady who does our curtains and things over on the next block. She was just admitted to the hospital in a bad way and her physician, Dr. Harvey, called me to help out until she is well enough to care for her children herself."

"How did this doctor know to call you? Do you know him?"

"I guess he knows us from church and from Mrs. Davis. She must have had my phone number available in the house. Dr. Harvey knew from Mrs. Davis' oldest daughter that she worked for me. If we don't care for them then they will be taken by the state. Dr. Harvey said he didn't have anyone else to call. I hope you don't mind, darling. They will be under my care and you won't have to worry about anything."

Before Leonard could answer Angela continued, "Do you mind, honey? It will be an adjustment to say the least. I don't know how long it will be either? Mrs. Davis is quite ill."

"Sweetheart, whatever you have to do is okay with me. I know you have a kind heart and would take in a stray dog if it needed your help. It is fine with me. I don't mind. Our house is too big for just us anyway and it would be nice to hear the pitter patter of little feet for a change. Oh, by the way, how old are these children?"

"Well, the oldest, Clarinda, is ten and a real beauty with dark brown hair and beautiful blue eyes. Then there are Andrew, a handsome four-year-old with blond hair and green eyes and his baby sister, Brenda, who is only two. She is just adorable with curly blonde hair and pretty green eyes. Your heart will melt when you meet them. They are so precious and so needy. Would you believe that they don't own any toys or new clothes? Also, there were no signs of Christmas in their house. It is so sad for children to live that way. Their mother was having a difficult time on her own. I never realized that she needed help. I would have been more than happy to help if she only had asked me."

"I am sure you will do more than enough to help them now that you know they need help, sweetheart. It's good to hear you sounding so happy. I can't wait to get home to meet them. See you soon, Angela."

Chapter 7

Angela put down the phone and continued making dinner, mac and cheese, chicken fingers and mixed veggies. She wanted to make sure the kids got their veggies too. She heard the sound of feet coming up behind her and looked down to see the sweet faces of Brenda and Andrew and close behind was Clarinda. They were looking at the food with such longing that she told them to go wash their hands and faces and come sit down to eat. They hurried along to the bathroom that had been pointed out to them earlier and came back and sat down before Angela could turn back around with the food in hand.

The children were sitting down with napkins tucked under their chins and forks and spoons in hand waiting expectantly for their much coveted dinner. Angela placed a plate full of food in front of each child and stepped back. Clarinda jumped up and ran over to her sister's side and began cutting up her chicken and then moved over to Andrew's and did the same for him. Angela watched in awe as this young girl acted as if she was their mother. Once Clarinda had taken care of her sibling's needs she sat down and began to eat her own food.

The children were so hungry that they ate too fast at first and began to choke. Clarinda jumped up once again to aid her siblings and tell them to slow down and chew their food carefully. Angela sat at the other end of the table and watched as the children finished every last morsel in their dishes and drank every drop of their milk.

Angela asked them, "Would you like more food or milk?"

"No, we are fine, thank you, Mrs. Antonelli. It was very good." Clarinda turned to her siblings and said, "Say 'thank you' to Mrs. Antonelli, Brenda and Andrew."

"Tank you," said Brenda.

"Thank you," replied Andrew who smiled showing some chicken still stuck in his teeth.

Angela had to keep herself busy and grabbed the plates off the table to prevent her eyes from filling and spilling over in front of the children. She mumbled, "You are welcome, children."

Leonard had walked in quietly and had witnessed this unbeknownst to his wife. He noisily cleared his throat to get her attention. She rushed over to hug him and then introduced him to the children. They stood up and looked at him not sure what to do or say.

Clarinda broke the silence by saying, "Hello, Mr. Antonelli, nice to meet you. Thank you for letting us stay in your home." She walked over to Leonard and extended her small hand in greeting.

Leonard was at a loss for words and just reached over and shook Clarinda's hand. He smiled at her as she looked up at him with the most beautiful blue eyes he had ever seen besides his wife's, that is.

Clarinda brought her brother and sister in turn over to Mr. Antonelli and they both shook his hand too. Leonard wiped his eyes and smiled and said, "It's a real pleasure to meet all of you too. I hope you enjoy staying with us as much as we'll enjoy you being here."

Angela finished up the dishes and told Leonard that she was going to put the children to bed upstairs in the three guest rooms. They had five bedrooms and four bathrooms which they had hoped one day to fill. Now at least they would be using three of them. The children followed Angela up the long winding staircase to begin their unexpected stay at this big strange house. Their eyes got bigger as they took in the long staircase and all the beautiful lights above their heads. There were sconces all along the wall to light the way as they climbed.

Clarinda requested that they all stay in the same room since there were two beds in each spacious room which was more than enough for the three of them. She didn't want to be separated from her siblings and they, too, would not do well too far away from her. Once Brenda's head hit the pillow she was off as well as Andrew. It was the first time they had full stomachs at bedtime. Once Clarinda was sure her siblings were asleep she allowed herself to snuggle down under the warm, soft comforter and she, too, fell fast asleep next to Brenda.

Before retiring for bed Angela peeked in and tucked them all in and giving each child a peck on the cheek. She shut off the light but not before looking fondly one more time at each sweet face in the beds. She felt such a longing and a tightness in her chest that she thought she was having a heart attack. She realized that it was pure joy at finally having children in her home; something that she had always wanted.

Chapter 8

Angela flew downstairs to her husband and rushed into his arms as her tears fell onto his shoulder. He held her tightly and said, "Whatever happens, sweetheart, I promise you that we will adopt a child once these children go back to their mother. I see now how much you need to have a child and, I have to admit, I need one too. These three are very precious, aren't they?"

"Oh, yes, Leonard. I can't begin to tell you how happy I feel having children here. I have wanted to adopt since we learned I could not conceive. But I wasn't sure if you wanted to do that too. That would be wonderful! But for now, we should do what we can for these children."

"I pray that their mother recovers so she can take care of them. They truly need their mother." Leonard responded.

"I wanted to talk to you about that. Do you think Mrs. Davis would mind if we bought the children some clothes and toys? Maybe we can give this family the best Christmas they have ever had."

"I think we can manage that," Leonard said feeling the same joy as his wife.

"Tomorrow we will go out and start Christmas shopping for the children and decorate the house and get a tree and…. Oh, Leonard, I have never felt happier in my life all due to poor Mrs. Davis' getting sick. I pray that she will be well soon. In the meantime, we will give her children a home with us and do all we can to help her by paying all her bills in the hospital and on her house. No one should have to live as she did. Maybe she would like to live here with us. We certainly have enough room for everyone. We have so much to give and we need so little for ourselves. Up until now I didn't feel like celebrating Christmas and hadn't even bothered to put up the tree. But now with these lovely children I want to go all out and decorate from top to bottom."

"Yes, my darling, whatever your heart desires we will do. It is such a joy to see you so happy. But let's take it one day at a time. We don't want Mrs. Davis to feel as if we are trying to take over. She may want to go back to her own home when she is well."

The ringing of the phone startled them as they were lost in their plans. Leonard went to pick it up and raised his hand for Angela to come closer as she heard him say, "Yes, Dr. Harvey, the children are doing fine. They are all tucked in bed and sound asleep. How is Mrs. Davis doing? Do you know when she will be returning home yet?"

Dr. Harvey explained, "She is very sick but is coming around now and is taking fluids. I hope to see her feeling better by tomorrow in case you want to bring the children by for a little while. They will have to wear masks when they visit with her. We don't want them getting sick too. She asked for them as soon as she was awake. I told her that you and your wife were taking care of them. She was very pleased and said to tell you 'thank you very much for your kindness.'"

"Yes, we were just discussing that. We want to bring the children by on Christmas Day so they can celebrate the day with their mother. I will bring a dinner for all of us if you care to join us. Will the hospital allow us to do that?"

"I don't think they will but you can bring the children by to visit on Christmas Day. Mrs. Davis will be very happy to see them. It will give her an extra day to recuperate and rest. This is very gracious of both of you. Thank you. Well, I just wanted to check in on the children. Have to get back to rounds. Hope you both have a good evening and thank you again. Goodnight."

"You are very welcome, Dr. Harvey. Goodnight." Leonard hung up the phone and turned to his wife and nodded. "It's all set. We can go visit on Christmas but no dinner there. The children will be happy just to see their mother."

"Oh, well, that's okay. As long as the children get to visit with their mother. I am happy too. We can come back home and I will cook a dinner for us, turkey and all the fixings. I will put the turkey in the oven early that day." Angela smiled and twirled around as she felt her heart swell with all the joy that was bubbling up inside her.

Chapter 9

An hour after Clarinda had fallen asleep she jumped up from her warm bed and looked around and realized where she was but something wasn't right. Oh my God! She just remembered she forgot to bring Mrs. Antonelli's wash. How would she get paid so she could buy her family gifts for Christmas? She must tell Mrs. Antonelli.

Clarinda ran all the way down the stairs and stopped at the foot of the stairs when she saw the Antonelli's hugging and crying. She wondered what was wrong. Were they upset because she and her siblings were there?

She coughed to get their attention but didn't move. The Antonelli's turned around and were surprised to see Clarinda standing there staring at them and looking a little upset.

They went over to her and took her into their arms and hugged her. Clarinda hugged them back but was surprised at their gesture. She stepped back and said, "Excuse me Mr. & Mrs. Antonelli, but I almost forgot to tell you I finished your wash and left it at my house. Do you want me to go get it so you can pay me? I need to buy my brother and sister and mother gifts for Christmas."

"Oh, no, dear sweet child. There is no need for you to do that. I will go over later tomorrow and pick up the laundry. There is nothing for you to worry about, okay? We will take care of everything."

Clarinda couldn't say a word. She was shocked at what these nice people had just said. All she could do was cry and run into their arms and kiss them and thank them again and again but added, "Can we go visit our mother in the hospital on Christmas Day? I don't want her to be alone."

"Oh, dear sweet child, of course. We were going to tell you tomorrow about what we planned to do. We are going to go shopping for new clothes for you and your siblings and buy each of you a present to give to your mother for Christmas. You can pick out presents for Andrew and Brenda too. When we get back from the hospital we will have a big Christmas dinner with turkey and all the fixings."

"Before your mother gets home, we will go over to your house and decorate and buy some new things for your rooms and for your mother's too. We want your house to look like new." Angela had tears in her eyes as she explained their plan.

"Oh, Mr. & Mrs. Antonelli, this is the best Christmas I have ever had! Thank you so much! Now I can go back to sleep! I can't wait to tell Andrew and Brenda that we are going to see Mama and celebrate Christmas together. Good night and Merry Christmas!"

"Merry Christmas to you, too, sweet child!"

Angela and Leonard hugged and cried as they talked excitedly about what they were going to do and buy for the children and their mother for Christmas. They had never remembered feeling such pure joy. They gave thanks to God for bringing these children and their mother into their lonely lives. They vowed from this day on to always give to those in need not just at Christmas time but all the time.

Leonard looked at his lovely wife as she beamed with joy and said, "I often asked myself, 'What is the true meaning of Christmas?' Now I know, this is the true meaning of Christmas – giving to others in need. Not only will this be the best Christmas ever for this family but it will be the best one for us too!" Leonard put his arms around his wife and hugged her as they wiped away some joyful tears.

THE END

ABOUT THE AUTHOR

J. E. Spina is a retired administrative secretary from a school system in Massachusetts. She has always loved writing poetry and children's stories.

This is the third book that J.E. Spina has published. She has published eight children's stories and four middle-grade novels under Janice Spina. Janice is in the process of editing more books for publication.

J.E. Spina's logo is Jemsbooks for all ages, and her motto is Reading Gives You Wings to Fly! Her goal is to encourage children and adults to read daily to enrich their lives.

Look for more Jemsbooks on her website
http://www.jemsbooks.com

Follow and connect with J.E. on:
Twitter: http://twitter.com/janice_spina
Facebook:
http://www.facebook.com/janice.spina.9
LinkedIn: http://www.linkedin.com/pub/janice-spina/59/321/a01/

Janice also has a blog
http://www.jemsbooks.wordpress.com
Her blog is where she reviews books, interviews and supports fellow authors, writes about her travels, talks about her venture in writing and publishing and offers helpful information for authors.

J.E. Spina lives in New Hampshire with her husband, John, who is the illustrator of her children's books and designer of her book covers.

J.E. Spina loves to hear from readers and welcomes reviews from all places that her books are purchased. She says, "It's like Christmas each time I receive a review!"

If you would like to be on J.E. Spina's email list to receive updates, newsletters and special deals on books, please go to jjspina@comcast.net and put in subject line **JEMSBOOKS MAILING LIST**.

www.ingramcontent.com/pod-product-compliance
Lightning Source LLC
Chambersburg PA
CBHW071207260626
47162CB00004B/1202